I0676727

ISBN 978-0-557-60694-8

this book
Is
dedicated
To my mother

whom
without her hardwork
This book would
not
Exist.

also
to my Panera Café
1024,

my second family…

contents:;:

WARNING:

THESE STORIES YOU ARE ABOUT
TO READ

ARE OF MY OWN DESIGN.

ANY RELATIONS TO PERSONS
LIVING OR DEAD
PLACES OR THINGS
ARE MERE ACCIDENT
OR USED WITH PERMISSION

PLEASE DO

GIVE IN TO FEAR

KNOW THY NEIGHBOR

It was cold. An unnerving and bitter kind of cold that felt more like ungodly torture then weather. This is the third night in a row the freezing temperature kept me awake. That, or the realization that everyone was dying around me. It started when the power went out.

There's a scrap of decaying earth, freshly fallen snow.

Relax.

I pull he heavy green blanket tighter. I loose myself in the thoughts of death and dying.

Moving so far from home was both scary and necessary for me. "You'll love the country scene." my mother said. "Clean air will do you some good Sara."

Funny. A million miles from Chicago and I don't feel any better. Fuck this apartment complex and fuck this cold.

My eyes open and shift about in the darkness. I can barely make out my reflection in the mirror on the wall. The moonlight at this hour feels more like daylight. I can just make out the dancing snowflakes as they tumble past my second story window.

My brother suggested I move near DeKalb. He said the small town and campus life was just what I needed after the divorce. Blake was the one who found this place. Sunnyside Apartments. The brochure made me laugh. Computer plastered ethnics pasted amongst elderly couples moving in. Happy fools carrying taped up boxes.

It was cheap and affordable.

I was sold.

Moving into a big collection of apartments was daunting at first but I learned rather quickly that the neighbors were all about becoming like family. They were really helpful and friendly, though very overbearing and kind of creepy at first.

My eyes look at the shelf near the door. Books and pictures are haphazardly placed on its now dusty surface.

Growing colder. Pull the blanket with my legs.

I met Erik and Danielle on the first day. Danielle… She was so sweet and very reserved. I thought she hated me at first meeting, but it was just her character.

"I'd rather have people fear me then love me." She laughs, "…to think I intimidate people."

It was true. Danielle was a thin and short girl whose demeanor and energy was far from scary. After we talked a few times at the shared washing, I realized she was just one of those girls you have to get to know.

Once we had exchanged numbers there was always a chance at an invitation to hookah or bar hop.

"You only live once, cliché but true." I remember her lamenting just before downing a shot.

Danielle…she didn't deserve to go out like that.

Early winter and just a few days until Christmas. On a night of both ghastly winds and powerful snow falls, our shitty complex was struck by a disastrous hail. Either which way, fate fucked us by destroying both the power and back-up power sources for apartments.

McGregor held a meeting by candlelight that it'd take some time to fix. Three nights in and the first rowdies found Danielle Baker.

The cops said; well actually my neighbor Preston who happens to be a new recruit, that she must of tried taking a shower while heavily intoxicated and in total darkness. They say her head hit the tiles sometime after midnight.

Erik had warned me of Danielle's often drinking the first day we met. Boxes in hand, he helped me carry my things into the one bedroom space.

"Always stumbling up the stairs and past my door at all hours. Singing, screaming, sometimes even stripping." I enjoyed his sarcastic nature. "The girls just a mess sometimes."

Actually, Erik was the one who first told me about Danielle. Keys enfolded in my leather gloved hands, Erik shook me as I walked from my car. His sudden grip and voice calling for my attention rattled me. "I have to tell you something."

That's when I noticed the ambulance and the cop cars. Preston and McGregor talking across the blurry lot. Other people were drawn from their respective apartments. Mary, the elderly woman only living here until her training is finished. She was amongst a small cluster of people, including Preston's roommate Scott.

Erik's words fell cold and icy as he described to me about how he himself found that my closest friend had just been found dead. "I'm sorry." The wind snaps at the window. "You okay?"

Still his words seemed forced. Erik had always seemed to genuinely care for me. He would always help me when I asked him to, even offering to help haul old furniture away when he saw me struggling. But that day he seemed different. As frigid and emotionless as the snow, Erik seemed fake to me.

The wind knocks again, this time causing my nervous heart to skip a beat. I toss on my larger mattress and stare at my ugly wooden dresser. My eyes now fully adjusted to the bitter darkness.

Speaking of seeming different, Preston seems defeated. His whole outlook has gone from warmhearted and overjoyed to fearful and shaken. it was his roommate that was found dead next. Scott was a writer, and the rumors were him and Preston were faggots together.

Never met a queer, but it was clear Preston was. it was all there in the way he wore his uniform. All tight and short. Homosexuality aside, Scott was found in what appeared as another bizarre accidental death.

The kitchen, which was so small hazards seemed common, had a small pool of water all over the floor. Scott tumbled and found his butcher knife at the just the right angle to catch it in the ribs. There, a bloody mess, Preston found him.

"Damned idiot still had an unlit cigarette in his mouth!" Preston cried when he recounted his story for the police. He wasn't considered a suspect. Not after Mr. Pearson turned up.

I stare at my dad's old acoustic guitar. It's the only piece of him I still have. That and this god awful nose of mine. I never knew nor met Mr. Pearson but Mary was one of his only friends. He was a retired war vet. My memory traces as I vaguely remember one of Mary's stories about him.

Mary and I often did our laundry at the same time. She would recount the days of her youth as I usually pretended to listen. She was nice but it was clear from the way she talked that she was a mother, of three to be exact.

8

Pulling my arm out from beneath the sheets and I regret opening that can of worms, both in my head and in my memory. Mary never shut up about her kids. She missed them as her soon to be new job required her to train for six months in Illinois. Kentucky, born and raised girly.

Mary was okay, but my mother wasn't my friend and Mary couldn't be mine either. I jab the pillow to soften it and I remember when I found Mary sobbing on the stairs.

Putting down my dirty load of laundry I asked her what was wrong. She burst out in a crying and crippling voice that spoke of her raw emotion and pain. "He was such a nice man." She said he had taken the wrong medication. In the darkness Mr. Pearson tried to relieve some joint and wound related pain. Unknowingly he took a powerful dose of rat poison.

"The cops said he had the stuff all over the place." Mary wiped the tears with her sleeve. "He was always so paranoid. I think it's from Nam but whose for sure. The man may have had a few screws loose but he was still a gentleman."

I close my eyes in an attempt to fall back asleep and cease this calamity of thoughts.

I remember Tim.

The snow lightly raps against the glass, the wind knocking once again.

Timothy was found just a few doors away. Though on the first floor. I can still see the bright yellow tape as they circled off his final landing space.

Tim Woods tumbled from his second story balcony onto the icy and unforgiving pavement below. His brains now exposed for us to see; it was ruled again as an accidental death. The floor on his balcony was covered in a thick sheet of ice.

I tremble slightly as I imagine Tim's open eyes, staring on the ground at all the spectators. They're lifeless though screaming loud enough to make me sweat with fear.

My eyes close tighter. I feel a sudden cold grip my leg. I twitch with fear. Icy skin bumps rise up, an indication that the temperature is rising. That or I'm wrapping myself tighter in a thick uncomfortable blanket of fear.

The wind picks up. It slams against the glass, rattling the white wooden frame. Four people dead. I was still new here, the feeling of new neighbor paranoia was still unsettled. Now this? Who can I trust. When it seems these accidental deaths happen at the right moment.

Chance and fate are two sides of the same coin. Though this risky string of incidents seemed.

"Fake", I say to the silence. I readjust on my mattress. Sudden chill. The roughness of my dry skin under my cheek.

Suddenly my phone rings. The bright glow of the tiny screen calls to attention. Erik on the display.

"Hello?"

"You awake?"

"Of course." Could anyone sleep?

"Could I come over?"

The question raises the tempo of my heartbeat. Should I let him spend the night? Maybe having someone here could relieve the paranoia. Then again I remember his words. Forced and of bitter plastic. Erik Raymond was a handsome man. Fuck it, he was gorgeous at least to me. Before that day though. Now he seemed broken.

The image I lusted after had begun to flake away. I remember we're on the phone.

"Sara?"

I cough. "Yeah, sorry, yeah swing by I'm going to change first."

He laughs, "Alright, be there in ten."

Nervousness. Fear. the wind slams again. The phone line falls silent.

Should I have let him come over? I trace the buttons of my phone with my finger. I decide to text Preston. He was the one who first said he thought these weren't accidents. "Just not enough evidence."

Preston told me, teary eyed and shaken, that it had to be a resident. Someone as cold hearted as the winter. He became with this new thought. My fingers press the keys to ask if he's still awake. Message sent.

Three days of death and cold. Winter had always been my favorite season as a child but as the years pass the more I grew to hate it. Four bodies six day of gruesome discovery. Once they found Tim, my fear became insomnia.

Three nights of no sleep. I move my eyes in a slow circle. Moving them with the imaginary movement of my quiet ceiling fan. My mind is beyond exhausted. Bare and shallow, my thoughts can only retain their basic notions. I fear I'm driving myself mad.

Suddenly there's a loud snap. Quiet. I sit uncomfortable in the sudden emptiness.

My ears try and trace the silence. I listen for another noise leak. My fear hears hushed breathing. "It's the wind, it's the wind." My paranoia hears the hush sound grow closer.

It hears the phantoms lightened footsteps as they reach just outside my door.

"It's just the wind."

The emotion quickly turns to passion, the strong fear sending pin pricks down my legs. I try to quietly move from atop my mattress. A spring lowers and rises releasing a loud rusted crack. The breathing stops. My legs freeze just above the floor. "It's not the wind."

As the balls of my feet inch towards the floor, my heartbeat returns to it's symphonic rush of beats. Just before I stand there's a monstrous burst of force. The intruder busting through my bedroom door.
Shadowy movement, moonlight painting in slits across the figure. On my feet, heart racing. Fear. Unknowing. Shaking. Back against the wall.
The unknown stands, sees I'm awake. Takes in the entire situation. Moon catches metal. I see the knife gleam.
My hand feels behind me. My alarm clock, glass. Empty but for the few remnants of chilled water. Fingers grip. My muscles flex and the glass flies at my attacker.
It soars and shatters as it hits the floor in the hallway.
I move as the knife is flung in my direction. I can feel the air cut past my arm. Legs over torso, I tumble over the bed. Two more quick stabs with the weapon. Pain all over. My thoughts fly out scattered. The mysterious man looks as lost as I. I use the opportunity to run for my father's guitar. "I'm sorry" I whisper to ghost of him.

My fingers tighten on the strings. The heavy wood moves with me in a quick and powerful swing of my arms. Instrument meets with elbow, the craftsmanship and bone shattering. The splintering skips across my bed. A moment of unbroken thinking.

The unknown coughs. He staggers for a moment. Fear keeps me locked at the foot of my bed. Weak, shocked. My whole body shakes as I feel I'm completely powerless to stop my own death.

My vocal chords strain as I finally force out a harsh and silent shattering scream. I hear the reverb of the cold room burst out, the edge of the dagger illuminated in it's approach. Sudden bang on the door. "Sara! Sara, is everything okay?!"

Erik's voice booms in the hallway, a beacon of hope. Turning in my sudden rush of adrenaline, I make my way to the door. I feel the tiny tufts of air as the intruder takes their swing at me. Almost there and I hear the tear of fabric as my attacker catches the edge of my t-shirt. It rips along the sharp edge almost making me rip. Fingers lock around the door knob Shadows shift and Erik enters with a small light showing his worried face.

"You okay?" he says as he grips my trembling shoulders. I panic, "Look out, there's someone in here!"

In a quick and protective motion Erik forces me behind him. He moves his backlit cell phone about my small apartment. The tiny screen reveals my hauntingly empty furniture. No one in sight, my phantom attacker gone as fast as they came.

"You sure?"
"I promise you!", I cut him off. "Someone is in here."
Erik grabs my hand. "Well I'm here now, everything…." A crack in the floorboards. Echo. My room is occupied. He leans in close. My nose is hit with his alluring scent. My hero. I can make out his eyes in the moonlight. Cold.

"Stay here."
"I'm coming with."
"You have a gun?"
Stupid question. "No!"

"Stay behind me."

12

Another crack and a movement of wind. Silence. Heavy breathing. Fear begins to creep. The two of us move through the living room, down the hall. Darkness and icy chills surround us. I can almost make-out my breath. Looming blackness that shifts about and makes it harder to see. Erik showed up right in time. My heart still beating in rapid time. Then the silence is broken.

"I'm glad I came."
"Why?"
"Had to see for myself."

The wind taps at the window. What was Erik going on about? I didn't have time to answer, as we now stood at the door frame. Erik takes in a deep breath. Silence.

Then he begins to hum. At first the song is unknown. The beating of my heart beats in my eardrums, giving the song its cruel backbone. As we step into the room I can just make out the notes to "Mary had a Little Lamb."

Erik seems to forget me as he moves about the room. With his light fading in and out his song repeats. I pass the handle of my guitar, I question picking it up. Continuing is uncomfortable he stands before the closet. He grows louder as his hand reaches for the handle.

"Whose fleece was white as snow."
Knock, knock, his fingers rap against the white wood.

Erik turns to me. "You can come out now Mary."

What's going....

My closet door pops open. One black suited leg steps out. In a sliver of moon my one-time attacker stands, almost proud to have been found. Leathered hands pull off the black knit cap covering her face. He shifts from fear grown beast to humbled mother in an instant.

Confusion. Fear not subsiding. What's happening.
"I'm surprised." Erik says. He begins to move slowly towards me. "You do good work."

13

"And I would have been finished by now if it weren't for you!"

I am desperate to scream and to demand my questions but my nerves strangle my voice. I am quiet and contained in all this sudden confusion. Mary is a killer? Erik seems real now. Twisted dark but real. Was he in on it? Did he know more then he let on? My brain pulses with painful misdirection. What do I do?

Erik sits at the foot of the bed. "And what Mary, you make it look like a suicide?"

Her eyes move wildly. She grips the knife in her hand as she unravels. "Yes! I had it all planned out. Suicide note and everything."

"You mean this?" His hands unfold a snow covered letter. I can catch my false signature at the bottom.

Mary lunges, "How did you..."

"You dropped it." Erik stands. "I knew someone enjoyed my work. After that messy job with the cops boy toy, I knew I'd have to meet my copycat."

Copy....

"You couldn't have all the fun! It was too easy. After I watched them wheel out that drunk, I said I could do better."

"But you almost got me caught!" His anger filled the room.

"Better you , me."

His hand sails through the air, smack. Knuckle to cheek. Erik slaps Mary sending her to the floor. "Don't be a dumb ass." The knife slides near my locked feet.

"I had planned out how to kill those idiots, timed the finding of each body. I even chose who to save! But then, some stuck up, insane housewife comes along and thinks they can just do better! Because of you my work is tarnished! They still haven't found half my work!"

Anger. Fear. Sorrow. My mind buzzes. What am I involved in? Cold paranoia. I'm useless. A child in a web of disaster.

"They haven't even found Mr. McKnight or Paula and Greg! You are so fucking stupid! How dare you! And now..." His heated eyes turn to me, "We have this one! What do you intend to do with her now?"

Mary stands back up.

I try to move but I stumble. Erik runs over. I try to scream but I can't. Before I can even muster a plea for help Erik's powerful arms wrap tight around my torso. I move about trying to break free but it's no good.

"Well?" Erik asks coldly.
Mary moves closer. She is no longer the warm hearted mother I once knew. In the midnight glow she drew closer, a monster. Animalistic in her lust to kill.

Muscles tense. Fear. Aggression. Why won't they just let me go?
Erik pulls me up. Out two bodies lined tight, Mary looks me and the room over.

"We can still do the suicide thing. I can clean up the room."

"After the police hand cuff us? We need to move fast." His hand grips my throat. "This one screamed loud enough to wake someone I'm sure."
Mary paces. She looks at the guitar on the floor. Her left hand rubs the back of her head as she plots my death. If they're going to move fast, I need to move faster.

Unknowing the wind is still. Darkness enveloping this tormented scene. Flash of light. My cell phone rings.
"Quickly grab it!" Erik orders. His hand moves to point at my distracting device.

Now's my chance.

Crack! In a sudden moment I whip my head forward and back. Erik's forehead is cracked open as he tumbles back and into my mirror.

15

Free. Adrenaline. Seconds. Think!

Mary charges but I duck down and just out of her grasp. She topples over me and hit's the wall with a thud.

Move.
Legs loosen up.
Hand grips knife.
Running for the door.

I hear movement behind me. Sudden, angry movement.

My feet slam against the floor as I use all my strength to run as fast as I can to the door.

Darkness. Someone reached for me. I tumble.
As I twist I bring the blade around.
Metal slices flesh.
Dagger meets with bone.
I stick Mary right in the gut.
Blood, or what feels like it, pours out on my wrist. Warm, I swear a stream of steam dances out.
She screams. Gurgles. I push her over.
Keep running.
I get back to my feet. As I do I see Erik's silhouette in the door way.

"Stop!"

I run.

I hear his heavy footsteps behind me. His breath at my neck.
Before he can grab me, my door bursts open. Sudden wind. Cold. Light.

"Freeze!"

Preston stands, his flashlight blinds me. I slip and fall at his feet.
Erik soars past me. The two men tumble out my door and into the bitter winter.
Gun shots. silence. The two men roll down the stairs. Heavy breathing.

Fear.
I get to my feet.
Step out into the freezing air.

The two bodies lay motionless at the bottom of my stairs. What do I do?
Movement. Someone is getting up. Preston! He moves Erik from atop him.
I almost fall as I run down the stairs. Preston saved me! I grip his cold
hand and help him to his feet. Erik's lifeless body stays on the ground.

"Are you okay?"
He fixes his uniform. "Been better."

We move a little ways from the landing space. I catch Preston's
nervousness in the moonlight. Cold and the wind suddenly cease.
Motionless, Preston stares at me. Fear holds my thoughts once again. What
do I say?

"What happened?"
I move my chilled lips to speak but I see sudden movement. Just behind
Preston, Erik stands up like a reanimated corpse.
Moonlight catches gun.

"Look out!"
My arms shove Preston to the left. Flashes. Gun blasts. Bullets just
miss. I hit the ground hard.
Erik gains ground. He steps closer. He doesn't want to miss again.

Preston helps me up and we move.

Erik fires again.

A cry of agony. His shot hits Preston's shoulder.
We run.
Barefoot I run along my apartment building.

Erik laughs in madness.

Preston keeps his grip on me, keeping me moving. We reach the back of
the lot. The dead generator near us!

"Stop!"

Preston pulls me towards him.
We turn to face Erik.
Blood paints his stomach and face. Matted, his hair blows like a beast in the wind. He aims the gun at us. My eyes move from him to behind him.

Fear. Fear. Fear. My thoughts are painfully focused.

"It's over Erik." Preston says as if he's unsure. "You've got no ammo."
"Don't think you can fool me, faggot!"

Fingers lock. Click-click.
Gun shots fire.

Preston aims his smoking barrel at Erik.

He stumbles.

I didn't even see Preston get out his gun. He returns it to the holster on his back.
Erik steps forward. Crimson spit flows from his lips. His eyes cold, afraid. He falls back. A loud crash as he slams into the power box.

Burst of electricity.
Sparks fly.
The lights flicker on.
Erik gasps. Cooks.

Preston covers me. I look on.
The lights shine long enough to catch Erik's final moment.

Biter. Cold. Defeated.
His eyes gloss over as the lights fall silent.

There, me and Preston stand, staring at a man we both never knew. A man we lived with for months.

Snow falls. Relief. Calm. Warmth.
Preston holds me, tears escaping out, both of fear and pain.

The apartment complex falls back into silence.
We wait as the sirens draw close.

-end-

THE LONG NIGHT AHEAD

Shawn smiled with bright white hope as he stood before the bathroom mirror. Quietly he looked at his thin frame, examining his tiny imperfections. Shawn Richards wasn't overly concerned with his looks but today there was a strong thirst to fix himself. A deep weight pressed onto his shoulders. It demanded recognition, to be a sickening string of thoughts that tainted Shawn's mind.

All at once, Shawn's faults were burning center stage. Every one of Shawn's freckles and every difference in skin tone sang a tormented melody of disgust. Shawn hated how he looked. Suddenly there was knock at the door.

Moments fluttered through a hazy filter as Shawn finished his morning routine. The brief moment of self loathing was an escape from the daily mechanics Shawn consumed himself in. It was easier with out the dangerous and inferior processing of emotions. Shawn cared not for such things to tangle up in his head.

Shawn had found that this heartless view of life had left him with the ability to dig deep into the twisted blackness of evil. With it he can spin stories that are on the edge of sanity. Each tale speaks with a powerful truth, painting with the words a void in which fear and disgust birthed.

His school's newspaper was looking for short stories to print in the entertainment section. Weaver High School's crypt master was a very bizarre man. A principal with an eye and ear for everything macabre. Shawn's writing was the thing Dr. Haines was thirsty for. And with great joy Shawn spun his world's for two dark years.

Now that Shawn was in his final year he had to leave Weaver High with one last scare. for days he had heard quiet whispers about what his story might be. After the shocking first piece "Sally Was A Lover", his school welcomed the dark and tragic tales with wet anticipation. Each month the students would wait to read the next road Shawn chose to travel down.

With graduation practice underway he could hear his classmates talking. There was a subtle hush of Shawn re-exploring one specific story that struck a powerful nerve with the entire school. It was a disturbing account of an enigmatic psychopath and the game of cat and mouse he plays with an unsuspecting family.

The story, though the ink is fresh with terrifying originality, it hit very close to home. it fell on the month of April, the same time Willows end experienced similar tragedy. Though the murder which happened many years ago, the sheer fact that it happened has been a strong thorn in everyone's side.

With shocked eyes the student body devoured "And I Was Watching." The title involved the same murderous view from the real killer. Shawn had told the story with great passion for the material. Every line ached with the terrible truth of what happened.

The hushed gossip said the sequel would follow the surviving family venturing out from the home and all dealing with it in cadaverous rage. Shawn's friend in his Gym class always asked about a sequel. "With delighted ears his friend Josh waited for the tiniest bit of information.

"Dude just tell me. I know you got all these other stories to finish first but, man. Are you thinking about it?" His voiced animosity boomed through the sweaty weight room.

Josh had also gained "strong" notion that the story would have the surviving mother going to California and opening a flower shop. For a while that's all Josh had said to him. Shawn wondered what his fellow mates thought. Was Ms. DiCiamo not affected by what transpired.

Did everyone think he was going to bail out and not give them one final scare but rather, a prank? The days Josh refused to continue on added to the boiling thought of his work being nothing but a joke.

Finally Josh broke with the story, the ending to a tale that tormented a few. Ms. DiCiamo uses her flower shop as a cover for her cannibal hunger. She used the left over parts for pottery or soil. Shawn laughed.

"Are you serious? She eats people? Why would I go that route?"

Josh shrugged as he continued to pump iron. "How should I know? Don't you only have a month to think about it? Senior issue man"

Shawn didn't know what to say. He was right. There were stacks of stories he could choose to publish. Dozens of tales about things no one else could possibly imagine. Deep down Shawn knew they were weak. they lacked that feeling of real terror as you read.

For the following nights Shawn sat reading over his stories, again and again. he explored deeper and farther along the layers as characters he created.

Every time he read over the tarnished words he felt that he ripped away a piece of realism. The more he spoke with these false personas the more their jaded likes were revealed. Shawn couldn't publish any of these pieces of garbage. Sitting in his car, the dusk spiraling into the limelight, Shawn had to think of the perfect story.

Claire looked radiant in the drifting sun, her blond hair falling elegantly past her shoulders. Her smile brought comfort in Shawn's unsettling situation. It was the one thing that could bring weight from the possibility of failing off the tipping scale.

Tonight he had to make the final decision but first he needed a moment. He decided to take his girlfriend, of one year, on a movie date. She had never gotten him to see a romantic film with her but he promised her this one night. Entering the looming theatre was only the beginning.

As the clean and mediocre scenes flashed away, time skipped a beat. Shawn's thoughts sat torn between love and his passion. Claire's warm touch soothed him but still the crying voices of his characters burned. Which story would he fix up and give to the friends at the newspaper.

Shawn wasn't one to hang around with a club or organization so he didn't consider himself a staff member. His eyes stared with a dry force at the massive screen before him. Soon the music would grow with a poorly written end with the empty darkness of the credits following to release him from this moment.

Everything that had been presented did nothing to quiet his questions. The vast catacombs of tales that hung across his brow was gathering into knots. Stories began to slip into each, other villains facing off, heroes dying before their peace.

Claire saw none of this as she drifted into the movies shallow plot. As they drove to her home in silence she didn't see the fear on Shawn's face. Claire looked out the window and into the night sky.

"You picked a story yet?" she questioned loosely.

Shawn gripped the cool wheel tighter. his eyes pierced through his headlights. "I have to send it in by midnight."

"So that's why we saw an early movie," Clair laughed. "I'm glad you did that for me."

She twirled her hair and placed a hand on Shawn's, grasping his fingers with the warm slender grip of hers. The voice of Erica screamed out from behind the running water. Her hand held to shield the attack from Shawn's curious thoughts.

The story of the murderous husband who gets rid of his small family and hid it for years. The tale of a twisted man with a face of was, who fooled the town into believing every poisoned work he spoke.

Shawn's vision of the silenced street was beginning to blur. Claire again chose to ignore the subtle signs Shawn was exhibiting. He had to figure all this out. The imperfections he had taken the time to notice earlier sang with the choir of darkness.

The scar above his hip. Every random beauty mark kissed upon his skin, They were pressing deep with Shawn's imagination. They were growing with a macabre fixation, becoming more haunting and disgusting as

Shawn thought on.

"Shawn!" Claire blurted out as her hand gripped the dash board before her and the handle of her door.

With a sudden and thunderous scrap of his brakes, Shawn brought the car to a halt. The two had sat in a hushed vehicle, Shawn a victim to his sore thoughts. He had completely drove past Claire's house and was headed straight towards the massive bend around the curve. Where her house sat was the only thing that bothered Shawn about their relationship.

It sat on the end of the street, it's yellow side touching the beginning of a dangerous curve. There were countless encounters with crazy drivers who weren't paying attention. Shawn took a deep breath before looking over at Claire.

"Sorry."

She too, held her breath for a moment before saying, "Thanks again. You should try and get some sleep."

Clair opened the door, left an icy kiss on Shawn's cheek and exited the car. Shawn watched her as she moved away from him, her hair fading in the fresh moonlight. Love was the one fleeting emotion Shawn let consume his time. And it was only with Claire that he experienced it.

Tonight he has to just get his final scare ready. After that he will be free. No final deadlines, no more chewing at the bit. At least not until it was actually published. Then Shawn would have to deal with the terrible reality or the public view.

Once out there, his story would become open bait for any and all kinds of childish criticism. Shawn had a good thing going but a parasitic voice that always held doubt seemed to speak up. He never knew how his peers would take his words and this was his last chance to speak them.

The darkness of the road seemed to linger out for miles. Shining with a phantom glow, Shawn's headlights led him towards his home. Heavy weight began to slip across Shawn's wake, bringing with it a feeling of fatigue.

There she stood. Her frame was thin, her eyes held out the blazing desire to be saved. Every orifice began to ooze with a subtle crimson. Shawn watched. She begged and pleaded for a savior but the color of her life enticed Shawn to continue to watch.

As her mouth opened nothing but a harsh wind escaped. With the haunting roar came headlights. The burning yellow pulled the phantom woman apart, bringing Shawn back to reality.

The screaming air turned to a loud and ear splitting horn. It's powerful sound shook Shawn, his hands slipping over one another. Every ounce of Shawn's tiny car began to tumble, rocking every which way. He tried to gain control but his heart made it a struggle.

Finally, as quickly as it began it stopped. Shawn's wheels released a monstrous cry as it met with curbside. The car was tossed up, Shawn nothing but a doll tied to the seat. As the car met the earth, it finally rested.

Shawn stared at the open road ahead of him. How did he manage to get this far? As the lights fizzled in Shawn placed himself, his car now dead just on the outskirts of town. Shawn could see the lights growing distant. In the mirror, his town was now a small speck. He was sitting and trying desperately to figure out his next move.

In a dazed stupor Shawn must have missed the turn to get him home. Without even noticing Shawn had driven to the quiet cornfields that skirt his town. The wind made the small field dance and twirl; off in the distance he could see light.

There was one house on this street. Claire had showed him this country road on night. As houses turned to shady business buildings, that too changed to beautiful crops. Now in the still moonlight the vast plain looked almost menacing.

With a throbbing pain tensing his left side, Shaun got out of the car and checked for any damage. As his feet hit the unforgiving pavement, he realized what he'd hit. There was no curb out on this dirt dusty road. Shawn saw the rustling field before him shift into a mocking tone.

The tiny line of barbed wire that traced from the unknown object to Shawn's feet was enough to send him into a rage. His mind got flooded with anger and frustration. With blood heating to a boil, Shawn slammed the car door. Moving down, he grabbed at the mysterious trap and winced.

Soft and weak, the flesh on his hand met with sharp metal pain. The barbs dug deep but in his state of passion he cared little. Still, Shawn tried to pull the heavy weight and again the blade's hurt. In the dimming but still visible moonlight Shawn examined his hand. Tiny puncture holes began to weep blood. The brilliant red trails spiraled down his wrists.

Mary crept up closer to him. His mind pulsed as he sat there in the street. The bare footsteps that inched closer went in macabre harmony with his backbeat pain. Tiny razor-sharp pebbles scraped the surface of Mary's tired feet. Skin peeled slowly and her hands trembled.

Shawn's phantom image kept approaching. Soon he could feel the battered woman's tortured breath on the nape of his neck. The skin raised in little bumps as the cold-heart caressed Shawn's fear. Mary was nothing, only a figment but that didn't ease Shawn's heart any. As if her presence shook him fierce, Shawn scrambled to his feet.

His bloody appendage painted out his panicked path, tumbling into the driver's seat. As the image broke away from him, Shawn began to make his decisions. Looking through the darkness of his car's tomb, he searched for his cell phone. In practiced rhythm, his fingers pressed the numbers to reach Claire.

The static voice of her answering machine sent a jolt of frustration through his head. It swept over his back and across his shoulders. Shawn gripped the wheel with his right hand and dialed another number.

Having parents who were overly concerned about his safety worked in Shawn's favor. Though it would have made the process easier if his father would have just given him a spare tire to lug about. Shawn only half listened to the OnStar voice that was beginning the long wait for help.

The Woman had the monotone but emotionally overjoyed voice that was like sand paper to Shawn's ears. Shawn knew his car was resting on Vocal Road but he couldn't tell the help exactly how far along he was. Each word of the conversation felt like the volume was turned low. The high hiss of static made it numb, each sentence carrying less weight as they came out. Shawn's thoughts couldn't be pulled away from his work.

Not tonight. This was his last chance to show everyone the true meaning of fear.

Again a haunting choir of voices broke his concentration. The person on the other end of the phone was now white noise to the sounds of screaming. Erik Rogers of 'Summer Lane' stood before the car. His hands were bloody from his insane antics. Shawn never liked Erik. The man was created as a splitting image of his father, a labor of hatred that created a character so much like Mr. Richards that it warmed Shawn's heart.

He hated the man on paper more than his father, something Shawn never saw coming. As the tiny droplets of crimson slip past Erik's fingers, the cold blood that slowly dried on Shawn's hand now called attention. He pulled the phone from his ear to check his memory.

Though the gashes itched with pain, Shawn had all but forgotten. Concerned and slightly confused the woman on the phone tried to end the conversation. She told Shawn someone was on their way before releasing him from her attention. Shawn's min burned and pulsed.

He couldn't remember a word he said to the helped. His hands felt as if tiny tears of acid danced all about them. What in the world had he hit? Something in the pit of his stomach told him to get out and check. The harsh wind to his right told him to stay. Hands wrapped in pain trembled harder, setting the nervous backbeat to Shawn's beating heart.

Did he hit a piece of wood wrapped in barbed wire? That's the image and memory that came forward. He can hear it as it rebounded across the street, the scrapping metal of the trap scratching lightly. With his mind full of clutter he focused his eyes forward. There where that bastard Erik stood was the timber weapon.

As if fate were mocking him, the moonlight beautifully glistened off the sharp barbs. In disassociated movement, Shawn slammed his fists on the steering wheel. As fast as it happened, Shawn's vocal chord trembled as he released a powerful scream. The sounds burst all around him, hitting the glass of his secluded car and adding to his inner chaos.

"You forgot all about me."

Shawn's voice cut off. As his eyes peered before him he could hear her breathing.

"Look at me."

His eyes tried to focus on the number of his mileage but his ears demanded attention. That broken voice, full of sorrow and spite, belonged to Rebecca. "Look at me!"

Shawn couldn't. Soon the foul stench of rotting flesh went into his nose. Tearing at his senses it made Shawn's vision blur. Her breathing was getting harder and harder to ignore.

"Jonathon! Look at me!"

Remember the story. Shawn retraced Rebecca's story, trying to displace himself from this moment. Rebecca was the victim of love both lost and tormented from his most recent story 'Chill'. Rebecca was a beautiful women. Hair that radiated with elegance. Skin smooth and soft. After a high school reunion, Rebecca found herself torn between two hearts.

"JONATHON!"
Shawn focused.
He could see the faces of his characters. Derek , her husband of four years, was starting to slip away from her. Rebecca could feel the coldness of their dying romance. She knew that given the change, she'd dispose of her husband. For eating her heart and then daring to find love in another. That's where Jonathon came back into the picture.

He was the guy she had always dreamed of having. Just being near him was enough to make her ache with raw emotion. In that poorly lit ballroom the two reconnected.

Shawn could hear Rebecca's destroyed bones breaking as she drew in closer. Crimson echoed a metronome as it dripped onto the control panel between them. Shawn quickly moves his hand to the door handle. She screams.

"Don't leave!"
With a sudden flick of his wrist he pulls on the handle. As he falls on the wretched street Rebecca reaches for him. Her decayed hands stretch, the mold and peeling flesh cracking. Jonathon had you killed, dead by the end of the reunion. A spiked drink did her in. The scent of tainted fruit punch left a mark on Shawn's psyche. He shook his head. The tale faded. Headlights.

Moving fast. Laughter escapes the open window. It's the ghastly crew of 'Hell's Boys' coming to play chicken. Tired Shawn gets to his feet.
"Run boy! Run!"
The engine roars. They're not real. Both figment and undead haunts playing deadly tricks on any who travel down the dirt road. Forgotten by time, Hell's Boys met their fate in a dance of gun fire with long time rivals Skull Crew. But this wasn't their road. This was Vocal Road. The headlights grew. Shawn pressed to remember reality. Imperfections flaked over the tainted images. Monstrous horn and the ghosts vanish just as they drive through the now trembling Shawn.

Now emotion leaks. Shawn now knows true fear. His mind was playing cruel games on him. He was now certain the wooden trap from earlier was a figment too. He steps away from his car to once again examine what burst his tires. The demented object rests in the envious light. Still real. Tired now dead. Shawn releases a low hum before resting his head on the hood of his truck.

"You alright boy?"
Startled. Fear pulses again.
A man in overalls and a beat up trucker hat stares. His eyes alarming and fake as glass. Shawn didn't see him approach. He wasn't a figment.

Or was he?
Shawn couldn't be sure.
The man fixes his hat. "You call for help?"

Tripping over his nerve wrecked throat, Shawn mutters a quiet "Ye...Yes...About ten..."
"Well I'm here!" the man says, his wrinkled face twisting into a smile.

Shawn looks over. A rusted and badly damaged tow truck rests just behind his car. Blames the high wind on the unnoticed approach, still Shawn his unsure if this man is real. He's had a busy day at school, his mind now over worked. He was having trouble keeping reality straight.
Coughing into his hand the man looks over the scene. His skeletal frame moves into the street. He sees the wood plank dressed in barbed wire. Stepping over to it, he bends low, prodding it with his gloved hands. "This what you hit?"
A ghost moves just to the outskirts of the cornfield. Shawn feels their cold glare burning at his back. He responds before banishing the figment away. Like acid, these moments of insanity burn. The strange gentlemen picks up the wood, the heavy lumber seeming light as air in the man's possession.

"You in high school?"
"Yeah."
"Play any sports?"
"No."
"You a theater queer?"
"No."

28

"Math Team?", the man's voice strains with disappointment and a hint of frustration.

Shawn fixes his hair. His mind keeps transfixed on his assignment. "I'm on the newspaper staff."

"Oh. So you're a reporter?"

"I write stories every month."

"Isn't that a reporter?"

With a quiet scoff, Shawn replies, "These are fictional stories. A hundred percent made up. Like a monthly comic only with words." He laughs a nervous laugh.

In the rising moon the unknown helper again moves into the street. Erik Raymond crosses him. Their eyes seem to meet. Erik turns, fades, gone. Shawn keeps his eyes on the man. He feels the weight of failure press. His deadline creeps closer.

"How much for the tow?", trying to move things along.

"What kind of stories you write?" the man completely ignoring his question.

Fear beats again. Rebecca moves into the driver seat. She weeps for attention. Shawn tries again to regain his calm, control the situation. Feeling his nerves once again Shawn answers the man. "I write scary stories. Horror bits."

"Horror stories huh?"

"Yes and I have a dead…"

"You got any?"

Shawn is confused. "Have any…"

The mysterious now a little flustered. "Stories! You have any stories?"

"Now?"

His hat pulled low, the unknown lets out a low, raspy laugh. "Yeah, you got any?"

"Not…not at the moment."

Cold grip on his ankle. The traveling spirit has crawled up. Her molded eyes gleam with sorrow, her prom dress tattered and blooded. 'Requiem of Susan' was a bust. Shawn remembers every harsh criticism on what people called 'a desperate bail-out from a tired writer.' Or worst of all,

'Not even scary.'

Shawn kicks looks his sanity. The man begins to play with the two by four as he paces near his tow truck.

"I got one."

Again fear tenses every muscle. Emotion unchained seeps through Shawn, causing a riot of bottled up humanity. This fear was becoming too much too handle. He could feel his teeth clench and his skin tremble.

Chewing on his lower lips the tired old man begins to spin his story.

"Live here many years. Seen a whole lot of changes. Things people couldn't even imagine. This place ain't what it used to be.", he clears his throat. "Now, they say that there's a hermit out round these cornfields. A forgotten ole soul who preys on the foolish.

The moon shifts. The man continues to spin, the fear growing inside Shawn.

"People say this mad hermit leaves traps for people. Kids, teens, boys just like you on the road", he laughs, "Well, just like this. He waits. And when an unsuspecting fly wanders into his web, he snaps! Joining their soul to the forgotten just like his."

Relief. The man's tale was very cliché. Almost rehearsed. Shawn's inner thoughts muse about how long this old trucker waited to tell someone. Shawn was unimpressed. The fear began to melt away.

"You believe that?" Shawn only half asked. He didn't expect the old man to reply with a 'yes'.

The man stops. "You don't?"

Shawn crosses his arms. He smiles as the man draws close. "I've written scarier stories than that. Actually my little cousin told me one that gave me more chills than that. Sounds like a bunch of urban legend garbage to me."

The wood hit's the palm of the stranger's left hand. His eyes lock with Shawn's. "So you don't believe in my story huh?"

Joy. The man's pathetic attempts to scare Shawn were childish at best. Of course this ignorant fool thought it'd be easy to win. Shawn was helpless out here and helplessness feeds into fear. The two of them all alone on this out stretched road. Tiny lights flickered in and out of existence. Shawn knew what story to write.

"It's a good thing you don't believe."

Shawn's train of thought stops, the chosen tale still coming to fruition. "Why's that?"

"'Cause you'd have prolly of started screaming by now."
With that, Shawn's mind cracked. Skull meets with lumber and metal. Blood paints the street. One quick swing and Shawn's world fades to black. The winning story now exposed in it's fresh crimson ink, shining in the moonlight. Shawn lays quiet and motionless. His long night draws to a close.

Two days later and Clair's just arrived at school. Her face still worn from the constant crying, she steps into a hushed sea of students. Eyes would meet in her direction, pity and sorrow on her face. No one really said too much to the saddened soul.

"Claire." a voice calls to her.
Pete, the head of the news team. A stand just behind her with a stack of freshly printed news.
A bit shaken, Claire asks, "Is that the Senior Issue?"

There's a small sign of worry. Pete looks down at the tiny print. On the back of the collected stories is a large portrait of Shawn. His name written in bold black, Clair begins to feel the pain and sorrow creep again.

"I wanted to warn you." Pete explains. "Dr. Haines said to run the story. I tried to keep it…"
Claire almost collapses. As Pete's voice turns to static buzz, she weeps. Tears pour from her porcelain eyes as she gives in and falls to her knees.
Shawn was concerned about the final words and tale he'd leave his graduating class. Now in a painful stab of irony his final moments leak out. Shawn would have never guessed his death would be the final scare.

His last story, was the story of the year.

-end-

SKIN

Mary O'Ryan stood. Her room was sunken into a quiet calm. Looking into the mirror, Mary begins her self destruction. Scissors dance slowly above her flesh. The sharp and painful blade moves just above her soft flesh. the pressure grows. The dance increasing in movement, tiny gashes of crimson joining the macabre habit.

Mary has never liked herself. For seventeen years Mary had fed that awful beast of self loathing, soon falling into dark obsessions. If her anger would not subside, the pain would help her forget at least.

The lines of her inner hatred now bled in the reflection. Perfect in their twisted beauty, the gashes on her thighs were stabbing at Mary like pin pricks. She quickly wipes them clean before getting dressed.

With imperfection on her mind she checks herself again in the mirror. Her plain pink t-shirt and blue jeans seem fitting. They speak to her, saying that this plain, boring girl was who she was.

Doorbell breaks her train of thought.

Paula had arrived.

Grabbing the bloody scissors and towel, Mary tucks away her self inflicted sin. With anticipation and nervousness in her heart, Mary runs down the stairs to answer the door. Her footsteps echo through the empty house.

The door slowly pushing open Paula greets, "What's up, bitch!?"

Mary let's out a warm cry of joy before embracing her best friend. She lets Paula enter, taking off her shoes before heading to the kitchen.

"So how long will they be gone for?"

Mary sits at the kitchen island. She pulls her seat close to the small sink. Paula goes through the cupboards, carefully taking an inventory of Mary's food supply. Mary's parents made sure to stock up on all of her favorites before going off on their fifteenth honeymoon.

Her stepfather whispered to Mary as he stepped out the door, " I hid an extra hundred in the cookie jar."

Paula opens the fridge. "How long?"

"Oh…two weeks." Mary feels the soothing pain of her sin scabbing over.

Munching on an apple, Paula moves about the small kitchen.

"So you excited about tonight? I know I am!"

Mary shrugs, "I guess."

Sensing a case of Debbie Downs, Paula cheerily proclaims, "The party's for you, you have to be a little excited."

Deep down Mary was sure she felt some sort of excitement. The tiny ping of joy was silenced by the screaming voices of worry and doubt.

Paula was Molly's best friend, had been since grade school. Paula's beautiful blond hair had always made Molly a tiny bit jealous. It wasn't until she developed and her blonde became the cherry on top of her appeal. Molly was stuck in the social shadow of Paula's radiance.

Last week Paula forced Molly to try out for Poms at their high school. Being captain of her cheer squad, Paula said it'd help her get out of her shell. The failure of not making the cheerleading team made Molly envy Paula more.

Reluctantly Molly tried out and made the team. The other girls even stated that had real potential.

Paula was pleased. Molly wasn't so much.

She had always felt the B to Paula's scarlet A.

In her opinion Poms was just the squad of failed cheer hopefuls. The B to Paula's A-team.

Of course Molly didn't let Paula see any of this. She used her habit to make sure Paula was kept jaded.

"I told Brent to bring Thomas!" Paula said as she threw away her apples core.

Molly tenses up. Thomas Peterson was on the Lacrosse team. In his off season, he would often spend time at the local teen center, where Molly would volunteer.

Though the two went to the same high school and even volunteered together, Molly had always been too afraid to approach him. The most conversational thing ever offered between the two were only awkward hellos. Molly remembers the gash she gave herself the night she tried to ask him out.

Fool she thinks as her fingers trace the welt on her shoulder.

"Please don't tell me that's what you're wearing?"

Molly can sense both the sarcasm and direct criticism in Paula's voice. With her very bright blue eyes Paula judged Molly's laid back outfit. Molly had been so preoccupied with her nervous sin, she hadn't done her make-up or picked out something to wear. Now looking over Paula's gorgeous top and revealing skirt, Molly felt truly over shadowed.

"I told people this party was going to be hot. In that outfit umm...it could get warm but you're the main event Molly!" "You've got to look smoking." she said, her over joy sort of annoying to Molly's thoughts.

Molly flicks the faucet off and on in quick flick of her wrist. "What

34

time is everyone coming?"

Pretending to wear a watch, Paula gazes at her bare wrist. "I said eight but you never want to wait last minute."

"Do you think Tommy will come?"

She smiles. "Brett said they were both free. Come on, let's make you pretty."

The quiet comment stings Molly. It may have been fired in a hushed rush as Paula forced Molly to her feet but it echoed over and over.

-Let's make you pretty-

Clothes and accessories littered the tan carpet. Paula was busy teasing her hair as Molly debated between two tops to wear. Of course Paula had the final say but she wanted to see what Molly felt looked good. Both options had been picked by Paula, her recommendation being that classy but sluty would win Thomas over.

Molly's fingers caressed the soft turquoise fabric of the sequined halter top. It's thin veil of beauty was only worn once before. To Paula's graduation party to be exact. Her best friend had mentioned it being her favorite. The warm color really brought out her eyes.

A gentle wind moves the sultry red low cut shirt in Molly's other hand. it spoke of lust and aggression. The inner feelings Molly often hid would speak out in this revealing number.

Molly's older sister gave it to her before she left for College. Molly had never gotten around to wearing it. Something told her to wear it.

"I like this one," she says as she aligns the outfit to her image in the mirror. Someone different. A bold Molly who can look just as pretty as…

"Blue suits you better."

Her voice is like chalk board being defaced.

Molly turns. "I've never worn this."

Paula stands. She walks over to Molly. She begins to play with Molly's hair. Her icy fingers pull and form her long brown locks. There's a waxy smile that filters over Paula. Her fingers stop holding a large chunk high above her scalp.

"And you think tonight should be the night?"

"Yeah ." *-Positive-*.

"Me too." Her words, hollow and forced.

Paula releases Molly's hair. She returns to her large make-up kit. Brushes and pads throw tiny tufts of glitter to fly about the bedroom. Creams are whipped and pressed to warm and smooth flesh. The glow of a radiant snow is brought out about Molly's face.

Working like a professional Paula descends onto Molly. Colors are spread and painted. Imperfections, though few, are quickly hidden away. the two girls laugh in their childish ritual of doing each others make-up. Molly only fixes Paula's eyelashes as Paula came already dolled up.

"I love your complexion."

-Is she serious?-

"You've got this glow. It's almost supernatural."

"Ha ha." Molly pondered if Paula was being serious.

Paula moves a prickly black brush across Molly's cheek. It tickles. She coughs into her hand.

"I'm serious Moll. You remind me of Snow White." Paul laughs.

Molly feels a wave of sincerity and embarrassment. She had never even dreamed of comparing herself to some beautiful fairytale princess. Let alone someone else. Even if it was coming from her best friend. Paula was never the type to shoot out compliments. She was usually the one receiving them.

Random strokes with another brush, Molly smiles. "Thank you Paula."

"I envy you. Seriously, jealous. The red brings it out."

Molly catches herself in the mirror. It was true. There she sat in her black skirt and ruby red top. Her was curled and sculpted atop her head. Her face was bright, almost like the new moon. It was as if she was a completely different girl. She hadn't noticed her self hatred dissolving.

There was a knock followed by heavy laughter at the front door. Molly was pulled from her image. Happy to feel so beautiful.

"Someone's here!" Paula almost squealed.

The two girls jumped to their feet and screamed. Tonight would be an amazing night of untamed joy. They were free to let loose and let life take them away.

They squeeze before the mirror, looking themselves over one last time. Paula and Molly, red and white, both felt like movie stars. Nerves pouring all over them. Their smiles were almost frozen in place.

"Oh wait!" Paula runs over to the bed. She grabs a blue plastic bottle. "Glitter!"

With a snap she flips the purple top, squeezing out a shiny lotion onto her palm. Molly, washed in an ecstasy of sudden excitement, offered her hand. The two girls lathered and laughed before running down the stairs to greet their guests.

The night had just begun.

Liquored lips and cigarettes spoke of unrestricted fulfillment. Boys and girls dressed to kill all enjoyed the abundance of man made sin; their hearts content filled shot after shot. It was a noisy crowd that Molly quickly got lost in. There were so many people, so many faces skipping past.

The plastic lights strung up in last ditch efforts were the few sources of light illuminating the full house. Molly was enjoying every ounce of happiness that was now seeping through her pores. She smiled on the inside as she sang along with her fellow classmates. Rain drops no longer stormed her thoughts.

"Where's Tommy?"

"Hey! Molly", long and dragged out she heard it. Brent's voice beckoned her.

Red up in hand, Brent smiled and embraced Molly. He smelt of cheap cologne and vodka. Rosy cheeked, he told Molly about what a great time he was having. He was spilling over with thankfulness for being invited.

She laughs "Really. It's my pleasure."

Then she sees him. Thomas. he breaks through the crowd in the front room. Tiny in number, the few kids that formed the dance floor swayed nearby. Thomas drank from his red cup. He smiles.

"Hey Moll."

-Moll....

"Hey."

Brent leans on Tommy for support. He lets him rest on his broad shoulders. "Great party."

"Thanks."

"I'm glad I came."

"Me too."

He smiles. A release of regurgitated air, Brent burps before getting lost in the crowd. Thomas moves in. Nervousness once again pulls on Molly's paper heart. She's already weak. His scent is the midnight air.

"How come we've never hung out before?"

"I don't know....common interest?" Nerves turn to cockiness as they're exposed.

Intrigued. "You ever hear of Frisbee golf?"

-*Cute.* "Yeah"

"You like it?"

"I guess."

He smiles. "There! We like a few of the same things already."

Molly is a little shocked. Was Thomas really hitting on her? Flirting? Tommy Peterson. She smiles. He gets closer, leaning on the couch behind them.

"So you working the big picnic at the teen center next week?"

She hadn't planned on it. "Yeah, if my schedule lets me."

Thomas shrugs. His eyes scout the room. "Well if you decide to go, let me know. I can give you a lift."

"Thank you." *Don't let it be the end.* - Her mind races.

She tries to continue the conversation. Molly wants to avoid that always awkward silence.

"Say Thomas..."

Wrist, hand, leg, thrusting girl. A girl jokingly dances on Thomas.

"TOMMY! OH OH!" the girl shouts as she thrusts a few more times.

He's unimpressed.

Ramona Benson stops her brotherly love before striking up a conversation the quiet Molly fading out.

"How you been Tom-may?"

"Good. How you been Benson?"

"Good, Good. You know, working out a lot. Making that money, you know what's up." She laughs.

Molly starts to move away. She feels a warmth on her wrist. Nervousness.

"Hey....wanna dance?"

She looks into Tommy's eyes. They're soft, inviting. There is a small sense of security. Benson scoffs. Pulling Molly close to him, he begins to lead her to the dance floor. Molly's heart beats in rapid succession. The high pitched beats of the music are in nervous time with Moll's pulse.

"Hey Ray, could you hold this?" Tom says before handing her his near empty cup.

Molly laughs. She catches the angry face Ramona's now wearing. Her eyes pierce towards Molly. She feels the wave of jealousy. A soothing movement was washes away some of the nerves. Tommy's grip on her hand tightens as he wraps his arms around Molly. She hopes he doesn't notice her tell tale crush now thumping loud and clear.

The two move and sway, the lights flickering down on this perfect moment.

"You look gorgeous."

"Thank you."

He moves in. Molly can smell the sweet scent of his being. She embraces the warmth of his touch. The music swells as her heart skips a beat.

Paula enters the room. Molly catches her watchful eyes. The best friend smiles. Brent runs over to her, pulling her towards the loud music. The two dance, moving towards Molly and Tom. There is a strong feeling of relentless passion. She chokes on this still afraid of Tommy and this moment not being real.

The four are enticed by the sounds, drunk on their raw emotion, lost in a spiral that felt like ecstasy.

"Let's get a drink." Paula whispers.

Molly smiles. She knows Paula wants to talk about the boys. With excitement she gets close to Tommy's open ear.

"Be right back."

Thomas smiles, still warm and inviting. He mouths the letters "Ok" and starts to jokingly dance on Brent.

The two girls move into the almost empty kitchen. Molly had been dancing so long and with a drive to keep going that she lost track of time. Paula was already moving quickly to grab various liquors and things to make the two host a much needed drink.

Paula talks with her back to Molly. "Nice moves out there."

Molly leans on the island. Her eyes look out into the sea of people. "Thanks. I love Cobra Starship."

"I wasn't talking about your dancing," Paula shoots her a smirk.

"Oh...Tommy."

"Yeah! I'm so proud of you. Going in there and getting what you want. I knew you had it in you." Almost mockingly.

Her heart stings with pain. Molly hadn't really done anything but be herself. There wasn't any game or string she was trying to use. She spoke the true words that kept leapt from her heart. Or at least where she believed they came. Molly had only said a few words. Tommy did the pursuing.

"Yeah...I guess." Molly dances. She sways in her emotion. She remembers Tommy's touch. "He made it easier. He acted like I was hard to get or something. Like I rejected him!"

Disbelief. Paula continues to mix her and Molly's drinks. She laughs a little. "Thomas took lead? He wanted you?"

Pain again. Molly stands. She stares had into Paula's back. The friend continues to mix liquids. Sounds of tops and bottles opening and closing are heard softly behind the music.

Paula turns, two cups in hand "This is a great party. Seriously to us!"

The cup is offered and accepted. Molly stares into the swirling potion. Hues of red and black move in a perfect circle. The two girls press their fake smiles before swallowing the hard mixture down. Rancid and bitter as all hell, the liquor burns Molly's throat. Already her head swells with frustration.

They make their way back to the dance floor. The music pounds along the walls. Molly feels hands all about her. Sinful contact from persons unknown. Vibrations from the heavy bass that invades her every pore. She feels the liquor start to take control.

Poison man made is demanding immediate attention, from all over Molly's body. Joy, sorrow, anger all wash over in a messy tide of emotion. Paula grabs onto Molly's hand and pulls into the screaming crowd.

Molly's eyes roll about, the lights becoming sickening lines of neon blue. She closes them to try and relax. Her heart races.

Thomas greets her.

They start to dance.

The music swells.
Paula laughs.
Her heart beats louder.
She feels his warmth.
Music grows intense and Molly's world fades to black.

Immense pain. Powerful burning pain. Like acid it shoots all over.
Every inch of Molly's being is engulfed in pain.

She tries to scream, too weak.
She opens her eyes and sees red. Nothing but red.
Sharp pain. Agony.
Her throat stretches and snaps. No scream.
She tries to move but can't.
It's a sea of red. Crimson liquid surrounds her.

The pain swells, grows more intense as she realizes she's in the bath
tub. The red is her blood. Her flesh freshly peeled.
She tries to cry, tries to scream but only feels deathly pain.
Paula laughs.
Molly turns to see her standing before the mirror.
"You still alive?"
Pain.
"I can't believe it."
Paula's naked.
"Well, at least you lost your virginity tonight. Won't have to worry
about dying a worthless loser."
Immense pain. Paula looks different. Alien. A monster.
She laughs. "Don't worry, I cleaned you up after Tommy had his
fun. Wouldn't want the new me getting dirty."
Death creeps up. Then it hits her. Everything about Paula is new
but familiar.
When the answer speaks Molly wants to cry.

Paula's wearing Molly's skin. She's fixing the pale wrists and glove
like fingers as she looks over herself in the mirror.
Breath like decayed flesh. Death is at Molly's ear.

41

Pain. Loathing.

"You see Moll, I never really liked you. I really only envied you."

Paula comes closer. Molly stares into her own Halloween masked face.

"Perfect skin."

The pain begins to numb. The red fading to white.

Paula laughs. "Don't worry, I'll take good care of it."

Molly sheds a final tear as her pain and hatred finally cease. In a pool of red she breathes her last breath.

-end-

THAT KILL

I wake up. Roll over, stretching across my queen sized bed. Light the spork, take the hit. The herb hits so smooth this early in the morning. I breath out and play with the second hand smoke.

Nine o'clock.

I got work in an hour. I stand and hap-hazardously get ready for work. Another day at the mall. Another day I jokingly compromise the thought of shooting up the place. My shitty beater van rocket me to work, the weed subsiding enough to handle the job ahead.

The clock ticks.
Customer walks in.
The clock ticks.
He heaves.
Tick.
Two girls walk in.
Tick. Tick.
They try on clothes
Tick.
They leave.
Tick.
I stare off into space.
Silence.
Tick.
Silence.
Tick.
Time seems to slow.
Silence.
My manager screams at me.
I let those two girls steal a bags worth of goods.
Tick.
BOOM. I laugh.
It'd be so easy.

Sitting out on my break I take a long drag of my cigarette. I think. Would life be this shitty if everyone smoked a little pot?

I wasn't always a smoker. Tobacco and weed. I hated the one since I could remember. Memories of drunken nights where my father smelt of bar. He strikes my mother in the figment.

I pull on the cigarette.
But then I got to High School. Smoking sticks helped with the stress at home.
I exhale.

Weed? That was help and a half. It calmed everything. Made the misery of life easier to handle. Those feelings of fear, worry, doubt; they're tossed to the side. Or at least quieted enough to get work done.

There's a kid and his mother across the parking lot. He screams, his arms thrashing in angst His mother shoves him. I smile. I wonder if I was ever that annoying.

Another drag.

I enjoyed smoking. The herb at least. Unlike tobacco, I didn't get that pain in my throat and lungs. And that feeling of habit wasn't spoken. Smokers always seemed like burned out souls to me. They wear each cigarette in the darkness under their eyes and dryness of skin.

I wonder if I too look like them. Living Chimneys.

I exhale.

I kill the smoke half way through it's life and take a short walk around the lot. Cars jet past me as I walk the aisles.

Marijuana never felt, nor feels like a problem. To me, it silences the voices that prevent me from getting through the day. I can just relax.

Sure I can get pills to do the same thing but to me that's self-admitted addiction. I know I'll grow to need it.

I don't need weed.

But I do enjoy having the option to partake in it. So many nights of good memories.

A car full of kids brushes past.
One of them catches eyes with me.
Smiles.
I smile back.

Life has been… well life. Before I started smoking pot I was a shelled turtle.
Overprotected.
Afraid.
Hermit.
I needed change.

Mari Jane spoke. She told me it'll all be okay. To stop worrying. To let go.

To live.
And I did.
I have been.

My dark days of self infliction, pain, and loneliness were gone. I basked in the dew of life.

I laugh.

I realize I'm thinking dangerously. Truth, but not the type of thoughts that I should put weight on.

Time's up.

I return to work. Once again that clock mocks me with it's quiet whispers.

As I put my cigarettes in my locker, my phone screams.

It shakes and rattles to tell me I've received a new text message.

"Gene Bean"
My dealer.
I flip open the device. He writes….
"Got that Kill"

My boss walks over, my hands lock up and I toss the phone away.

It'll have to wait.
Tick-Tick.
Got that kill.
Tick.
I want to smoke it.
Tick.
Tick.
Tick.

Driving along, music so loud the mirror vibrates.
Traffic is a cluster fuck.
Stop.
Go.
Wait. Change the station.
Stop.
Adjust the mirror.

The sun's setting.

My mind thinks about the night ahead. I have no plans and yet the unpainted canvas of tonight lays blank.

I call Ron.
"Hello?"
"What up dude?"
He coughs. "Not much man, just woke up."
"You serious? You are aware it's almost six o'half right?"
Ron laughs. "I worked a late shift last night, shut up."
"Whatever man." I pull ahead. Stop just short of a fender bender with the truck in front of me. "You got plans?"
Waiting.
"Nope. Ain't shit."
"You wanna smoke?"
Laughs again. "Of course man. Where?"
"Well I still gotta pick...about to do that right now. You wanna come with?"
Go.
Stop.
Dodge another incident.
Wait.
"Yeah man. You gonna scoop me up then?"
I laugh. Ron doesn't drive. No car. No license either. "No shit. Be ready."

I hang up before he says his peace. The sun is radiant. A beautiful image of life's wonders. The radio cuts out.

Static.
I drive.
Hands can't change the station.
Fuzz. Ghost noise. I try not to think about it.
Voices static.
Stop.
My hands quickly slam the device off.
Silence.
Sigh of relief.

Tonight should be interesting. Haven't had luck with the quality of the green.

That kill.

I smile.

Can't wait.

Ron drops his phone in the door's handle. It's been five minutes.

Come on Gene.

"So it's cool that John comes?"

"Yeah. Told Maggie and Alex to head over after work. I was gonna tell Andy when we got back." I grip the wheel.

It's not like Gene to keep me waiting. The sun is almost completely silent. No glimmer too bright.

"Where is this guy?"

Uncomfortable. We're both a little agitated.

"No clue."

He stretches out.

"He better not skimp out."

"He won't."

"You sure it's kill?"

I nod. Gene's never let me down. When he hits gold, it's usually legit. "I promise. You'll get high."

Ron laughs a sarcastic chuckle.

"You think they'll ever legalize it?"

"Fat chance. Too many powerful folks would loose out. Can't go letting the people gain while the ones in charge take a hit."

Confused. I know it's illegal for all the wrong reasons. Originally due to racism, now because it's a gateway. Or whatever else they want to believe.

"Too many people loose?"

He clears his throat, sits up more alert. "Yeah dude. While we, the voters or whatever, gain. You know, jobs, revenue, the medical shit. We would get a little better economically but!"

But?

"The people who loose would be alcohol and tobacco businesses. They, have been the quiet helpers of our little economy."

His words and claims were loose, wild at best. I could see it as mindless dribble but I know better. It felt like truth. How could legalizing something that does so much good hurt? It hurts in a theory of having no limits but until I see crack or ecstasy helping cure diseases or ailments, that's just theory.

We wouldn't have to legalize it all. We could create the laws that put the safety, the control, have it something that's ok but contained. It could work. I laugh.

The people in power don't care though. Another laugh. It's all just drugs and poisons to them.

"Where is this guy?" The distress in his voice clear.

The longer you sit in the same spot, waiting, the more time you give to getting caught. It's illegal. The pigs? They're "cracking down" which means tackling any teen who seems to happy or nervous to be behind the wheel.

"Gene's never like this man. He's always on time."
"Not tonight."
I place my head on the wheel.
Tick - tock Gene.
"He's a straight cat man. One time he hooked it up for the wait", I turn away from Ron. "I'm sure he has a good reason to make us wait."

Ron thinks it. He speaks it. "What it he got caught man?"
Not Gene. Too careful.
"Nah, he's too slick."
"They all want you to believe that man. Else you wouldn't buy from them."

Ron's right. If I ever had the tainted notion that Gene was "hot", that I could get busted messing with him, I would keep my distance. Got no time to waste getting busted. Can't loose it all. Even if the sun is still dirt.

"You think he's "dirty dealin'?"

Ron's eyes pierce into me. I can feel his nervousness. "No....don't say shit like that. I'm not getting busted man!"

Dirty dealing or whatever you decide to call it is when a dealer gets busted. Caught in the Legal bear trap he turns on his customers. He could help police find the users. He could sell out his men. The guys he buys from.

48

When it comes down to it, buying and selling drugs is a dangerous game. Seen lives lost over shit.

The minute fades to another digit.
Tick. Tick.
fear and paranoia in this quiet car.
Tick. Tick.
The night looms ahead as we sit in this darkened parking space.
Tick.
I check my phone.
It's been almost fifteen.
Tick.
"Gene, what the fuck?"

Usually when a dealer takes longer then ten minutes, I'd dip out and call him. Gene was different though. I only knew him as a dealer, nothing more.

He was plastic. A tool.
In my mind I couldn't put my fingers in grips. There was too much unknown and unsaid about the soul and persona that Gene Bean, dealer.
Head lights.
Roar of the engine.
He pulls up next to us.
"Bout time." Ron says
I look at him. "Chill aite? I'm payin' for it"
He scoffs.

Stepping out into the night the wind whips at my back. Quick movement and I get into his car.
Silence.
"Hey."
In the darkness, hands shift. No words. He pushes his goods into my lap.
Shifting again, shadows bloom, I hand him the money.

"This shit kill?", I ask.
Nervous.
I catch his eyes underneath the brim of this skull cap.

Cold. Shiver caresses my spine. Cold dead stare.

"Thanks."

I step out. Engine roars. Before my hand even tightens around my car's handle he's off.

The moon reflects on his windshield as he disappears. I sit in my seat uncomfortable. It didn't feel right.

"You get the shit?"

"Yeah."

He can read the worry on my face. "You alright?"

"Yeah."

Quiet stillness. "All...alright. To your place?"

Lost in fear. Unknown. "Yeah. My place."

"Dude you're scaring me a little bit."

His eyes scared me too. So dark. Like death's grip. I couldn't stop thinking about them. I turn my keys. Roar of the machine. So very cold. We head to my parent's place. Icy cold.

My fingers rub the plastic baggy.

The six of us circle up. Andy to my right, the ever gorgeous Maggie at my left.

John rocks back and forth on my Grandfather's old wheel hair. I laugh. The image of the many gained years, him at an older age is humorous. Ron puts his feet on a stack of old magazines.

"It's cool that we're all over this late?"

Alex is cute. She's sincere in her question. We had met a few years before but we just started smoking together recently. She was so funny once she got high. She came to life. Really, I could admit a small crush on her then. I laugh then answer.

"We're fine. Just smoke."

I return to preparing the small ritual. My glass piece lays lifeless in my lap. I open the tiny bag that holds our chosen sin. The aroma burst out.

It's pungent. Sweet and harshly bitter. Like a sour tart. It's a cruel higher then the ripest skunk. Everyone reacts.

"Damn dude!" Ron cries.

Maggie, fingers to her nose "That's some shit."

"Is that for real?" Andy asks in a ting of disbelief. "I've never smelled shit so strong."

Me either.

My senses almost couldn't take it. My entire garage was wrapped up in this scent of fresh herb. We all were excited to light it up.

I began to break it up. My fingers pressed against the lid. Like soft just. It was magic. Tiny green clouds almost that I tore apart so easily. I worked elegantly, gently as I filled the empty basin of Morgana.

She was a gift from my older brother last Christmas. She was beautiful to smoke out of and she hits like a beast. Good bowl size too. Perfect for a group this big.

Conversation infects the waiting friends.

Andy, "You think we could really die from all those pesticides they spray on the crops?"

"What makes you ask?"

"Ron was talking about metals in the water before. Made me remember this thing I saw about the pesticides. You know the shit to kill the bugs?"

Maggie laughs, "Poisons aren't good ever. Not even in the slightest."

"But we've been eating shit like that for years.", Alex adds.

"Doesn't make it any less dangerous." John rocks forward, at the center of our smoking circle.

Almost full. The leaves are so powdery. Very brittle. My skin has a tiny itch, like small pricks of allergies.

"If the shit they spray on our food could kill bugs what's stopping it from doing the same to us?"

Ron laughs. "Hello….?" We're totally different species. They're specks of flesh man. Tiny annoyances at best."

"So you're saying we're immune to dangerous toxins?"

He laughs again. "Yeah, a little bit. In the right does you could kill us sure, but the small clouds they spread on your mom's apples won't kill her."

He reclines. "Me?" I don't eat fruits."

Everyone laughs.

The bowls packed. I hand it to Andy. He's a little reluctant but he knows I don't take my own greens. I believe in Karma. Not good to be greedy on haters such as marijuana and a good time. It'll only hurt you in the end.

Embers sizzle. Morgana comes to life. She speaks. Andy is hit. Smoke coughs out.

A huge hit.

"Hey, it's Two-Hits-Tuesday!"

Maggie playfully punches me. "You made that up."

I nod. I look at Andy. His face is flushed red. He took a killer first hit. "Go ahead."

Again the embers dance. The snap and crackle of the sin is loud. Morgana hisses as she's passed to the right. Ron excitedly lights up. I look at Andy.

He's gone. Everything is different. There's a heavy fog of groove surrounding him. His vibe is toasted. Glazed over eyes a clear sign of him shooting off too far gone. I smile. This shit is what Gene said. Andy looks like he's been smoking for days. Soon Ron joins him.

As John speaks with Morgana, Ron flies away. Eyes nearly closed, he just laughs as the smoke he released clears. I can smell the power of the thc in the air. I can read it's effects, instant in theory, coming to life before me.

With the smoking piece now in Alex's hands the vibe changes.

Andy moans.

I look over.

His eyes are red. Really red. Almost ruby.

Tears shed. Only not clear salty tears. Slow crimson tears.

Andy's crying blood.

Panic.

Ron starts to cough.

Andy moans.

Maggie begins her turn, not paying attention to the agony Andy is beginning to experience from two hits of bud.

Ron spits as he coughs.

A tooth hit's the floor.

More red.

John cries as Ron fall forward.

Fear and smoke fog up mind.

Andy's gums ooze, gush, becoming rotting slop.

Ron coughs, chokes as he too cries the same red tears that Andy shed.

Alex. Sweet Alex cries too now. The smoke dancing about her angelically as she paints her face in red too.

My lap is gifted with the roasting bowl.

Maggie looks about the room. "Oh shit!"

"My stomach!"

Ron cries deathly bellows, "I...CAN'T....BREATH!"

John only creams. Crimson hues my view as I feel Maggie grab my wrist for support. Alex is silent in all her pain. Shock sweeps her body. It escapes in her eyes.

The smoke almost clear now. I put the piece before my lips. Morgana is eerily calm. Only a tool in this calamity. There's a glimmer of green. Fresh death looking back at me at the of this well.

My hand flicks my lighter.

Morgana waits.

My friends choke.

The smoke swirls around me. A fog of poison.

The scent entices me.

I got to hit this shit.

-END-

TRAIN WRECK

A clash of thunder. The rain so fierce it slams on the ground like bullets. Once again another day of glorious summer is ruined by the rain. Unexpected and sudden it was a change of plans for many.

Not for Erika and Kenny though.

They were not going to let a little summer storm ruin their night.

Not when they had been planning for the past two weeks.

With the drops of water starting as early as noon, Kenny was quick to see if anyone was no longer up for a drive to North Illinois Tech, the school Kenny left last semester.

His phone was filtering in the rings of Eddie's unanswered wake-up call.

"Come on douche…."

"Hello?"

"You up ass wipe?"

"Is it past noon?"

Kenny knows the drill. Ed Eckert never wakes up before one o'clock in the afternoon. Unless you call him several times, he won't wake up to answer.

"You still game for tonight?"

He groans. One could hear the ruffling of bed sheets. "Yeah dude. Why?"

"Have you seen the weather?"

With his room dimmed by heavy curtains, there was a comforting darkness that wrapped around the room.

Eddie responds. "Is it raining?"

Kenny kicks an empty cup towards the dumpster. He stares out into the storm behind his work. Tiny sprinkles of rain bounce off the protective umbrella.

"Like hell."

"Did they cancel?"

"Not yet. Henry did though."

Henry had called Kenny while he was still at work. Now that his shift was over Kenny took the time to listen to his voice mail.

The tornado warming up in Plainfield was too much for the pussy Henry to handle. He was going to play it safe and take the night to catch up on the homework. Kenny called him to try to convince him to still come along.

Sadie was having a party to end all parties. They couldn't miss it. Henry didn't care. He declined.

His let down caused Kenny to call both Keith and Erika, who were both, still down to go. Erika had just filled her tank. 'I'm ready to get fucked up!' he remembered her saying.

54

"Well as long as the girls are still having the bash, I'm game."

Ed had gone with Kenny to North Tech before. The two boys had spent the night wasted at Jessi Lorence's, Kenny's first college crush. Eddie spent most of his night in the bathroom.

He passed out with his arms hugging the toilet and his lips still kissing the seat. Kenny smiles inside remembering the hilarious image. He had really hit it off with Sadie's roommie Val. The two danced all night.

She had told Kenny he had to invite him to the party.

Ed was happy to accept.

"We leave at seven."

He clears his throat. "We got a booze fund going?"

"Erika was bringing an ounce of weed. Hadn't thought to pick up liquor."

Ed laughs. With one hand holding his cell phone, Eddie looks for his wallet. "Got my fake I.D. man!"

"Do you think that'll work?"

Kenny sees the image of the tiny ID in his head. He remembers seeing the fake when Ed had got it. He was so proud of the thing he went to four liquor stores to get celebratory booze. He purchased at all of them.

They had never really called upon it. Kenny didn't think it looked real. The photo was all off center and faded. The text of information was crooked. Though Ed had the proof that some people were fooled by it.

"Yeah. We can go grab a few things."

"I'm getting me some Jack."

Brown liquor, Kenny's mortal enemy. The stuff that left many of his nights blacked out. Jack Daniels was the king of those man made sins. He could feel the burn of the after taste. He swallowed hard. Ed was ready for another time like before.

"Let's not end up puking all night dude."

There's a sarcastic cackle. "One time. One time, due."

Rain drops seem to slow. The wind has died down. With only a trace left, the foggy hue of the day was beginning to fade. Kenny looks at his phone's clock. Only seven hours to kill. Plenty of time.

"Hey, I'm going to head home and shower. Erika's going to meet me at my place around six. She's grabbing Keith too."

He interrupts. "Grab the booze after you shower."

Kenny agrees. "See you soon."

"I'll be waiting."

The phone falls quiet.

The rain slowly continues to set the backdrop. Air as thin as satin blows. Kenny feels a chill creep up. He can't quiet the excitement in his mind or heart. He wanted tonight to be amazing. Tracy had promised to meet him at the party.

A secret love affair of two boys in a mad sort of love.

They walk the aisles of the small poison shanty. Many labels crave attention. Their many mascots enticing the patrons to choose them as their purchase. Kenny was silently nervous. He felt the handcuffs tighten on his wrists.

Ed was the one with the fake ID, Kenny felt it a ting unnecessary to have to go into the store as well. The "dangerous" kid knew his chosen liquor. Kenny felt stupid.

"You think I should grab us some SoCo? I know Sades loves the stuff."

Southern comfort was a sweet drink. Sadie was the one who had forced Kenny to try it out one drunken night. He had fallen in love with it's caramel flavor. He traces his memory and remembers it being Tracy's favorite.

Kenny looks out the huge glass panes to the outside world. The rain is still. A mere drizzle now. There was no longer that weight of major concern hanging over the night ahead. Ed walked over with two large bottles in each hand.

"You almost finished dude?"

Ed picks up Ken's concern for getting caught. "Chill out dude. I buy from here all the time. You're making me nervous."

"Just don't want to get busted. Not tonight."

He hands Ken one of the bottles of Jaeger. The blood drenched taste makes Kenny lick his lips. No good to him.

Gross.

"Had to make sure I had my wallet." Ed says as he grabs the liquor from Kenny.

The other customers in the store glare at Ken and Eddie. An older

56

woman and a newly wed couple.

Piercing eyes.

Kenny was more nervous

The two walked closer to check out.

With nerve shaken eyes he looked at the small collection of candies that were placed next to cheap vodkas.

Sour Patch Kids and chocolate bars made him remember.

He had met Tracy on Halloween night.

Dressed like the Spiderman.

He was doing beer bongs in the kitchen with their mutual friend Margie.

When Ken walked over he was wiping his face free of foam. it was cute. Tracy had that young, clean face. Smart but down to earth. His secret was Kenny's secret too. They could feel that forbidden intimacy waiting between the two.

Tracy offered him a bear bong.

Ken had only done it once before.

Tracy laughed. "Always good to practice."

After Kenny cleared it in less than thirty seconds, the two went on the balcony. The smoke was an added lust on the unspoken feelings. Ken can't remember who kissed who.

He didn't care.

Under the moonlight, there was a brief moment of bliss. Kenny wrapped himself in the memory of his scent. His warmth. The taste of his lips.

"Should I grab us a few blunts?"

The moment breaks.

He's back in the store. Eddies eyeing the flavors of their selection from the front of the check out counter.

"It's Erika's shit."

Ed laughs. "So? You think she's going to smoke it all?."

Kenny grabs a bag of sour gummies.

"Peach or grape?"

"Blunts waste."

He laughs. "But they're classy."

"It's smoking. Nothing about it is classy."

He asks for peach.

Ken walks over. The clerk shoots him a look. The same soul stabbing look the other people occupying the store gave before.

"ID?"

Kenny is shot with adrenaline. He's certain the clerk was asking him for a form of identification.

"Me?"

"Yes you; ID?"

Eddie cuts in. "Whoa, whoa, he's not buying anything dude."

The clerk senses trouble. He's not pleased. "I need ID."

Anger rules over Ed. It was ridiculous that this shop worker was asking Kenny for proof of age. He wasn't the one buying the liquor. Ken was just a guy standing too close to Ed at time of purchase.

"No way man. He's my younger bro. I just needed him to give me a lift."

The clerk's eyebrows raise. Only a small trace of family resemblance. Would he buy it?

"I'm buying almost fifty bucks worth of shit. You want the sale or not?"

Silent, defeated, the foolish clerk accepts the money and rings the two kids out.

As soon as the door to the store releases Kenny from the awkward moment, he laughs and cries in joy. The two dodged the bullet.

"Cool dude. Play it cool."

Ken gets in the car. The smile stained on his face. He can feel the clerks watchful eyes as he pulls away. Ed looks over the goods.

"Tonight's going to be fun."

Kenny remembers Tracy's soft, secret lips pressed to his.

"You bet."

Holding the bottle of Jack Daniels in his hands, Ed proposes, "A few shots before Erika and Keith stop by?"

He can feel the burn.

"Erika's driving. I'm game."

The two laugh as they make their return to Kenny's house.

58

They push the extra pillows into the crammed trunk. The bottles click together.

"Careful girl! Ed cries. "That's some precious cargo."

Erika rolls her eyes. She's not happy that the two boys opened one of the bottles. With so much green on her she was hoping to cut down on all the other possible risks. Keith honked the horn from inside the car.

"Let's go!" he cries.

The rain stopped.

The air was muggy. Thick with the freshly fallen rain. Everything was painted in it. Erika's hair was still wet from the water she caught before getting here.

"So we got everything?"

Ken agrees as he walks over to the passenger side of the small white four by four.

"You got directions?"

"Got that shit memorized Erika. Been there enough."

"But you've only driven up a few times."

It was true.

The two semesters that Kenny had spent up there he left his car home. Didn't want to buy a parking permit.

He opens the door. "We'll be fine."

Ed just shrugs before getting into the back with Kenny.

Erika gets behind the wheel, a trace of fear shines in her eyes.

"If we get lost Ken, I swear I will go back there and strangle you."

Kenny laughs. It's an empty threat from his best friend. The rain roars up with the engine. It picks up as the four teenagers pull away from home base.

Kenny keeps his eyes to the road. Keith tells the group about his recent dirt biking trip. The story cuts into Kenny's head.

The rain was quieted now. Not silent, only hushed. it was uncomfortable at best. Kenny looked out.

The roads were littered with furious drivers. All of them busy to get where they headed, as fast as they could. All of them wanted to beat the storm. Illinois was known for it's monstrous thunder storms. And with the open fields surrounding N.I. Tech, there was nothing stopping the great force.

"I'd wish this traffic would let up."

Keith excitedly looks ahead. "Man, you're really kissin that dude's bumper."

There's a quick smile. "Well, if he'd drive a little quicker, I wouldn't be."

Kenny ignores the conversation. Keith retraces the memory of a blizzard.

"Yeah, we had no idea. There we were, like up at the top of this….beautiful mountain peak. Snow had been falling all day and stuff but not as harsh as it did at the top. It was something."

Eddie shifts in his seat. "A tornado almost hit when I was moving in at NIU."

"There's tornadoes at Northern?"

"I haven't seen one." , he taps at his window. "I'd love to though."

"Hell yeah." Keith adds. "But I dunno if I'd wanna be right in the middle of one."

Stop and go traffic.

The car presses forward, quiet anticipation covers the group. With every stop of the vehicle, Kenny is rocked forward.

In this soft pattern. Stop and go. Stop and go. Kenny is rocked into a calm. A foggy calm.

"Where do we turn again?"

Kenny looked at the hidden signs, each one skipping past in the flickering street lights. He had been there before.

"Did that sign say 'Next Left Rocky Street IL 91?"

Emily is too busy watching the other cars to read each sign. Eddie had agreed to drive shotgun and give directions. Kenny knew he should have sat co-pilot. He moves his legs, get loose.

"Turn here."

She listens.

The roads are different. Unfamiliar. In the tiny fragments of rain a new suburb came into their view.

Kenny didn't know this place. They took the wrong exit.

"I don't think that was it." Eddie says, now unsure.

"God damn it Ed. What now? You think I know this town?"

Kenny looks out. He then looks over at Keith. His eyes are taking in all of the new territory.

"Been in a town like this. One summer when I was out surfing."

Keith grasps this situation. "Are we lost?"

Erika releases a playful sigh. Kenny can feel her frustration. "Now what? Do we call someone."

Eddie is busy playing on his phone. "Hold on."

"I don't have gas to be driving lost."

"Chill out."

Another lamp goes out. Kenny's counted four now. There is some sort of memory, false or dreamt up, that places itself here. He knows it isn't the right way but he feels like he should be here.

Stop and go.

They reach a busy section of the town.

Stop and go.

People doing shopping. Emergency or not, they were in their individual worlds. They too had places to be.

Stop and go.

"There. I downloaded an app" Eddie says proud.

Without his new cell phone the kid would be lost. It's no surprise that the soon-to-be-doctor had a nice, high tech device.

Eddie was rolling in cash, both parents successful doctors. Ed, with their money footing the bill, was chasing the same dreams. He loved the thrill of the ER. Taking chances and running risks to save lives. That rush of death gave Ed the drive.

"Good. Now get us outta this shit hole. Reminds me of the jobs."

The jobs.

Erika was a mortician. A would be hair stylist, she now makes the deceased pretty. Not her most pleasurable activity, others including books and poetry. She often reminded everyone she got paid to play with dead people.

Kenny feels a weight on his brow. A tired weight. He tries to keep awake.

Stop and go in the small town. But the weight starts to gain.

"You think the tornado'll hit once we get up there?"

"It's quiet now."

Stop and go. Traffic.

"Don't wanna die."

Stop. Go. Stop.

"Not tonight."

The weight is too much.

Slumber.

Willows sway, elegant in the gentle wind. Kenny walks along a narrow path, untraversed before. The trees wane in, grabbing closer to him. In this mucky, death like woods Kenny walked. Calm.

He knew this unbeaten path. With each step he grew with more anticipation. The sense of welcome waiting growing closer. Shadows in the woods walked along with him.

Beat. Beat. His heart spoke.
Midnight hum.
Readily quiet.
Beat. Beat.

The shadows that twisted and laughed in their macabre head, whispered to one another. A soft pitter patter of constant chat. Voices harsh but distant. So cold and full of falsehood.

Dropping down around Kenny.
Voices.
Pitter. Patter.
Beat. Beat.
The voice was distinct.
Direct.
Beat. Beat.

The rain quieted. Voices falling still with the shadows.

Kenny ran.
Feet pumping.

Legs moved in slow motion. He could feel his will to run, primal instinct to move fast but in this realm he was weak.
The voice counted down.

Kenny pressed forward. Distant lights come into the view.
Flickering hauntingly.
Kenny felt the familiar warmth begin to slither away. A dew of cold seeps over him.

The path grows out.

A clearing.
The voices chit chat. Soft again. Static noise.
Uncertain. Fear.
Railroad tracks.
And him.

The voices keep their monotone talk. A buzz. A rain.
A back fuzz to the man's speech.
Kenny felt the shadow and vice that poured from his words. Trying
to ignore him, Kenny was caught in a death lock stare.

The man was thin.
Sickly.
His flesh was gray. Rotting away at each layer.
Knuckles cut.
Hair thin and falling out.
A smell of a thousand corpses littered about.
Kenny choked on it.
The man turns.
His back moving like a fog.
So cold.
His eyes.
Burning eyes.
Kenny can't erase them.

The man continues to speak. Loud and with such fierce diction.
"You will rot in the flesh of the damned. Boiling infected skin will
bubble about your sinful body, screams so loud not even thunder can quiet
them."
"You will rot."
"You will burn."
His eyes never broke.
Kenny's heart leapt up.
Head lights.
A train was coming.
The man spoke louder.

Kenny tried to ignore the man but it was no use.
The man spoke.

The train came closer.
Loud as thunder the beast spoke.
Beat. Beat.
The voices whispered.
The train so close.
One quick yell of his voice,
"YOU WILL ROT!"

Jolted awake. Cold hand on his shoulder.

Keith shook him awake.
"Dude. You gotta see this."
The rain was present but distant.
You could hear it.
Almost see it.
But now the four drove in the barren country lands. They knew
they were getting closer.

"So...the rain..."
"Wait for it..."
Kenny pressed his eyes out into the almost darkness. He could see
in the moonlight a single farmhouse.
Crops pass.
Nothing.
Silent crops pass.
Kenny is growing out of curiosity "Keith man..."
Then flash.
Snap!
Thunder and lightning.
Night to day.
In a quick instant.

The bolt of nature struck. Loud and with an animalistic fury.
The four looked on.
"Damn."
Eddie replies, "You missed some good shit man."
"Been like this long?"
Erika swallows hard. "No and lets hope it ends."

Another flash.

Bright thunder light.

Kenny see a distant town.

It falls to darkness again.

"Damn it."

Kenny can sense Erika is uncomfortable. "Don't like the storm."

Quiet. The rain fills the static back drop.

"Not like this. Not like this."

Keith taps the window. "Man this is freaky shit."

Kenny agrees.

"I personally would find shelter as soon as this shit started. No sir. Fuck a tornado."

"There's not going to be a tornado."

"How can you be sure?"

Eddie laughs.

Uncomfortable, Erika continues. "Never been one in Illinois. Not one. So chill."

"Still....", Keith adds. "Perfect night for one."

Kenny speaks. "Wouldn't mind riding one out."

Another laugh from Eddie. Erika grips the wheel.

Kenny continues. "It'd be pretty sweet. Flying cows and shit." He laughs.

A sigh of relief from the driver.

Another flash.

Nothing.

Empty fields.

Desert almost.

The rain continues to whisper.

"Yeah, I think I'd like to at least SEE one."

Erika laughs, "Oh Mister 'Hide in a basement' here."

Keith laughs too. "Well, I'm just saying shit would be cool. I'd want to try and out run it. Just hit the gas and get to safety. Beat death almost."

There's an awkward jolt of laughter that flutters about. Everyone agrees that it'd be cool to escape death.

At least once.

"I don't think I'd want to die like that though."

Kenny smiles. "Well, me either but that thrill of just barely dying.

Man, we're talking twister man. Like epic wind tunnel that destroys buildings."

Everyone laughs.

Tapping the glass.

Flash.

Loud snap of monstrous storm.

Night to day.

Quiet.

"I'd open the window and stick my head out."

Eddie adds. "Shit, I'd try and get on the roof."

"Go out big."

"Hell yeah. If I make it out alive, great. If I don't, still went out like a bad ass."

Quiet rain grows.

Taunts them.

Flash. Flash.

Two bolts clash.

"No natural disaster death for me, thank you. I wanna go out old and with a hot nurse wiping my ass."

Ed only scoffs at Ken's crude joke. Erika and Keith roll in the laughter.

"Shit, sign me up for that death dude." Keith playfully jokes.

The car fills with laughter.

The rain is filtered out.

Flash.

Daylight.

Night.

Trees are seen at a distance. The various crops breath and exhale to light for brief moments as the storm continues.

"How long was I out?"

Keith laughs. "For a while. Your phone was going off too."

Tracy

Kenny frantically looks for his phone in the darkness of the car he can only make out the seat in front of him. Pitter patter of the rain.

Please, Tracy don't think I'm ignoring you.

His hands feel wildly about the floor.

Flash. Snap.

His phone at his foot Kenny checks to see if anyone's left him messages.

Seven messages.

Two missed calls.

Going through the messages and Kenny's world is painted to black.

Tracy called.

Sent him a message.

"People aren't coming out."

"Tornado watch. Too dangerous. Don't come out. Roads are closed up here."

Shaken.

Flash. Flash.

Kenny looked.

The trees were close. The pressed up against the glass. Listening to the sounds of the storm.

Rain soft as feather.

Tires pressing through muddy roads.

The radio was low now. It had stopped playing music.

Now only static.

"Damn, this is bad."

Static fuzz. Pitter of rain. Flash of electricity.

"I'm going to call Sadie."

His phone flashes.

'Please recharge soon!'

"Fuck."

Eddie feels his concern "You okay man?"

Flustered. His mind wrapping in on itself.

Static laughter.

Flash.

He tries to make the call.

There's a conversation started but Kenny can only hear the backtrack.

His phone beeps at him.

'Recharge!'

Static.

Thunder.

Rain

Trees scrape.

His phone dies.
Flash
Surrounded by looming trees.
"Guys…."

"Hold on…So, I had her against the wall right…"
Kenny tries, "Hey…"
"So she starts biting me and shit. Real Kinky."

Static static static.
Rain drops.
Quiet laughter.
Hushed sound.
Nervous heart beats.
"Guys, maybe we should …."
The trees and their deathly grip.

"What? Maybe we should…" Eddie says with a hint of anger.
Kenny finishes. "Maybe we should turn around."
A hideous laugh from Erika. "Too late."

Flash.
Slam.
Day to Night.
Life to death.
Flash. Flash.
Metal and flesh.
The train dragging the now demolished car for another block before
stopping.
Flash.

The red is painted on the tracks.
Simple.
Clean.
The rain is already present to help wash away another train wreck.

-END-

SKELETON MAN

My grandfather wasn't the most stable senior citizen. The shell shock from Nam really fried his brain.

So paranoid.

Of everyone and most of all a death he said was creeping on him every day.

In his sleep.

That's how he went out. Though I'm sure in his final dream there was a flurry of gun shots.

Him dying a hero.

The only thing I had in common was his name.

Richard.

My father was proud of his dad. I'm almost positive it's what made him keep his old man's run down home.

He built it himself. Him and a crew of his friends. This was before the war. Sure my dad grew up in it but when his folks split he went with his mother.

To Kentucky.

Leaving Boston to his past. Now here we are.

Standing before this falling apart hazard. My father excited as all hell to move in. My mother and sister carrying in boxes.

Me?

I'm still trying to swallow this fear.

I don't like this house.

Not one bit.

I walk in through it's faded entrance. It's shuddered eyes glare at me. Chipped skin and broken timber makes the porch creek hauntingly loud. Dust dances in the sun light.

"Excited to pick your room sport?"

Sport? He's chipper.

"Not really."

Sally bursts in. She throws her boxes down and dashes towards the stairs. "I get first pick!"

She's gone.

Empty and dead.

Cold and unwelcome.

"Better hurry. If I'm not mistaken one room has it's own bathroom."

I'm gone. My feet rush across the aged floor. I make my way up the spiraling staircase. Sally's jumping on an old mattress left from before.

"I get this one!"

I looked down the hall. Three rooms left unclaimed.

I make my way to the first, the smallest. This would be my dad's office. I see the desk in my imagination.

Next room.

The floorboards ache.

Master bedroom.

The size is extravagant.

It's own bath.

I leave disappointed.

Last room.

Round the corner and facing away from the rest.

I enter the dwelling.

Another door directly across from me. The room's decent sized. The closet's between the bathroom and the entrance. Memory of a visit.

This room is vacant.

Dirty as it was now.

I was younger.

Playing a game.

"Hide and seek Richie?"

Allison, my younger cousin begged. I closed my eyes and began to count. I couldn't find her. The last room. She had to be there.

I had been through the entire downstairs just prior. This closet hid my small cousin. she tucked herself behind a large box of old clothes. Her giggle broke the chilling silence of the room.

"Gotcha!" she cries as I slowly open the door.

Then I saw it.

The figurine.

His arms crossed.

His head hung low.
The skeleton man.

He lay imprisoned on the back wall of the closet. Not too large but still a creep big enough to make my heart beat with fear. Allison saw it too.
"What's that?"
Stunned. "No idea."
The tiny figure called to me. Kept me paralyzed.
Allison reached for it.
Just as her fingers grasped the damned doll my grandfather burst into the room.
"Stop!"
We both screamed.
"Don't you dare touch that!"
Allison runs from the room as my grandpa fixes the small bone collection.
"Don't you ever move this, you hear? Don't you touch it or else he'll come for me... and come for you too!"
He slams the door shut.

I'm back in the present dust. The closet looms before me. Fingers trembling I slide the door open. Smell of rotted wood and musky mold hits my senses. My eyes trace the closet. A box on the top shelf. Back wall bare. No skeleton man.
Just the empty back of the closet. I breath a sigh of relief.

My family's gathered downstairs in what we would assume to be the living room. Television set plugged in playing on of our favorite films. "Poltergeist."
Sally's clutching tight a pillow while she eats the fresh pizza.
"You really think we should be watching this? It's our first night in the house."
My dad laughs. He bites into a huge slice of pepperoni. "We watched it the last time we moved. It's tradition."
"Well let's hope tradition sticks and we don't move again." my mother says as she strokes my father's hair.
My mind is stuck on me leaving to start at a new school next week. Having to unpack tons of boxes. I ignored the clown that now blazed on screen. A large thump upstairs. My room. Like something fell over.

71

"Ghosts!" Sally cries.

Again my dad laughs. "No, someone just stacked some boxes wrong."

Shuffle. Shuffle.

Heavy footsteps.

Quiet.

"I'll go check." I say nervous and scared.

"Hurry back. the best part is coming up."

I make my way to the stairs. Each step makes my heart ache. Too quiet. Fear in each heart beat. I make my way to my room.

Whispers.

Dead whispers.

Like a haunted wind.

I stare at my door.

Something moves.

I push the door open.

Nothing.

Box of clothes spilled on the floor. I begin to pick them up. Dust dances from each piece of clothing. Something stirs behind me.

I tense up.

Red sweater tightens in my hand.

He draws closer.

Whisper in the stillness.

Heart in fear.

I shake.

Hands grip.

Rotted palm reaches out.

I close my eyes.

Flesh torn knuckles crack just above my shoulder.

It reaches.

I spin around.

Again, nothing.

Big sigh of calmness.

My hands back at my clothes.

Sudden grip of hair.

Hand turns over head.

Face mangled.

Eyes stare at me.

Centipede crawls from his decayed lips.

I scream.

It rolls about the floor.

I run down the stairs.

Make it to my now attentive family.

"You alright?" My dad asks now leaning forward from his seat. As if he's ready to heave. I breath deep.

"Yeah. Big spider."

I don't sleep in my room that night. I don't sleep at all. Ghostly whispers keep me awake.

The attic is covered in forgotten webs and mildew. A mannequin rests in the corner. Dozens of lost treasures sleep in the unopened boxes. My dad moves through the sea of them looking only briefly in each one.

I stand at the entrance. My nerves twitch. The sun filters in through the small window. It shines a light on the quiet dance of dust and old memories. Many unspoken questions and unanswered responses lay in the audience.

"What are you looking for?" I question.

My dad turns over a box. Photos.'

"Something son. Bring the light over."

He looks for his prize, not concerned with giving me any clue on what he was looking for. It's midday and there's no source of light up here.

Fear in my heart, nerves ache my throat. I walk the red flashlight over to my dad. My body tense. He fixes himself before opening a box. Dust mites and a sleeping spider scurry out.

I step back.

He smiles.

"Nervous?"

I shake my head.

A low chuckle. "Don't be. Ain't nothing up here but dust and mold. Uncomforting. Someone just before the entrance. Coming.

His eyes burn from the animalistic darkness. My father gives life to the flashlight and the darkness gets darker. The man gets closer. Again I tense up.

My dad moves cigar boxes, old receipts, junk all about the floor. The flashlight moves about. It flickers the light like a wild firefly about the attic.

73

It catches his face.

The same mangled face.

Darkness.

He breathes.

Light catches clothing.

Dressed Khaki.

Blood. Dried and rotted.

He exhales.

Scent of gunpowder, death, and I'm sick with a new fear. My dad opens a tin box. The thing stops moving. No breath. Silence.

With nervous hands he pulls out worn away photos. A necklace. With a locket. It falls unnecessary to the floor.

"Damn. Where you hiding you son of a bitch?" He whispers.

Nothing.

Figment gone.

No shadow.

My dad stands, almost defeated. he gives another scan of the attic. He too sees nothing. He walks over, the floorboards releasing a few cries of pain as he does so.

"See. I told you, nothing but dust and mold."

The man exit's the attic laughing to himself. I stand alone for moment. Only a moment.

And I could swear. In the stillness of the attic. In the hushed quiet. I swear I heard a whisper. The dead spoke out, "Murder."

My legs shook with a subtle frustration. Old habit was hard to kick. I laugh an awkward laugh. She paces about with a dust vacuum. Her clean almond green skirt flowing as she does her work.

"Don't pout Richard."

I'm not.

Just fuming.

My dad decided to host a sort of open house. He invited the entire block to stop by and get a chance to become acquainted.

I hadn't slept peacefully if at all in five days. School was about to start for me too. I didn't care for any of it.

Sally trounces in. Bubblegum slapping in her lips. There's a joy that sort of seeps from her. it turns my stomach.

"Chrissie and Paulie and Derek and Margie are coming over tonight! We're going to play hide and seek in the basement!"

My mother laughs. "You will do no such thing. It's filthy down there. There's bugs and spiders. Your father hasn't cleaned it out."

"That's why! It'll be scary!"

"I don't want you kids in the basement you hear? Off limits or you're grounded."

Stern. My mother didn't play games with matters. Her word was law.

"Fine." and Sally leaves the room. Her joy and youth quickly with her.

I fix myself on the couch. My mom stops her cleaning and heads into the kitchen.

"Your father invited Mandy and her younger brother Mark over. They're around the same age as you." She says as she pulls something from the oven.

"Joy."

The house looks more like a home. One dressed to party. But still, a home. In that appeal, that hollow facade lay fear. Tension and nerve.

It looked like a home but it felt like a prison. I walk up the stairs to take a shower. My mind ignores the weight of being watched. I try to focus on tonight though I hold no hopes. I miss my old house. My old friends. Stepping into the cell painted up like my room and I want to run away.

Get out of this house.

And a voice in the back of my mind whispers. *Before it's too late....*

The soft but harsh beads of rain on my skin wash away a bit of the tension. My heart is the steady drum to the noise of the shower.

Somehow I don't feel alone. I haven't really.

Not once since I stepped into my grandfather's old place. Like pulsing eyes were watching me. Always.

Unwelcome and cold. it made my stomach boil with raw paranoia and fear. The soap cleans away the sweat from my forehead. Somehow my arm brazes something sharp.

Cut deep.

A ribbon of crimson caresses down my side. I don't notice any pain. My eyes close tight to block out the lathered shampoo. I think about the night ahead.

"No."

"Set."

"Sally...don't I have to count..."

"Go!"

She's off and running. A few of the adults look over and wait for me to make my decision. There's a small tremor of unknowing trembling through my feet. I look around. Two of the kids ran upstairs to the bedrooms. Off limits but of course, those rules rarely stop the likes of children. Sally ran towards the kitchen. Maybe, if I catch her first, I can stop this whole game and get back to...

I remember that I have nothing in this new home. Just that feeling of unwelcome. He breathes deep at the top of the stairs. Eyes as cold as death. No heartbeat. Figment. Gone.

Hand on my shoulder. Turning slowly, I see that it's my new classmate Mandy. She's radiant in her green t-shirt and jeans.

"Hey."

"Hi."

"Need some help?"

I can't deny her.

We start to move about the party. Slow at first, making small talk. We're in the same grade. Sophomores in high school. Peter Blatty High. Only one class the same, but not together. She was taking a Theater class and in an advanced Math class.

"You good at math?"

"I guess. Makes more sense to me then English sometimes."

We laugh.

I feel the weight of the house on my shoulders. As we enter the dining room, I see movement under the perfectly placed table. A smile worms across my face.

"Thanks for helping me."

"No sweat."

"Did Mark come along?"

She moves to the other side of the table. "No, he's sick."

I give her a slight head nod and the kid is caught. She stomps her feet before moving into the kitchen for a cupcake. The defeated girl licks the frosting off the sweet with just anger.

"I know where Derek is hiding!" she claimed as she points upstairs.

"Shall we?"

The beautiful girl smiles and I'm smitten. We race upstairs and find the two kids amongst some unopened boxes and my parents closet. I learn that her and her brother are twins. She even revealed that she almost didn't make it out of the womb. A miracle of some sort and now she's here. In truth, I was too busy ignoring my fear of the house and the lust over her.

Mandy was something to behold in many aspects. I loved just being in her presence as she had a charm that she carried with her. I don't remember playing hide and seek really. I went through the motions. Suddenly, we were at the top of my basement stairs.

"Is there a light down there?"

I'm pulled back into the now. Sally was told to stay out of the basement but of course she went against the rules. All three of the other kids ratted her out, saying she wanted to go down there all night. The angel faced children all admitted to being afraid of the dark. No one dared go down there.

"Sally." I call to the nothingness.

She places a hand on my back. "Let's go."

We move quickly into the shadows. As if moving as fast as possible will help us conquer any fear we may have. I keep my hand against the wall as we move down the creaky staircase. Mandy holds close to my arm, not truly holding my hand, but close enough that the affection is still there.

A shimmer in the dying daylight and the low window. I see the string move about the darkness and my fingers pull tight. Suddenly the room is filled with bright light that soon fades to a mellow lamp. Boxes covered in dust and cobwebs are all about the small basement.

"Cool stuff."

There are various bikes and mannequins. Tools and collections that lay in random piles. So many things collected over my grandfather's lifetime. They almost all now lay forgotten down here. Movement behind us. Mandy turns abruptly, in fear and excitement. She wants to explore the shallow depths of this place too. I can't say that I don't feel the urge myself.

I try to remember that being caught by my mother would be the end of my freedom. She'd think I told Sally it was ok to be down here. But still the curiosity of my grandfather and who he was lingered stronger. My eyes pulled in so many directions.

A box shuffles my itself to my left.

I stare hard at the tall stack of unclaimed treasures. Amanda draws a little closer to me.

Sally jumps out with a loud roar. In her hands is the Skeleton Man. Only it's ragged. Tattered. Played with.

79

"Sally…"

Mandy jumped back a little when my sister attempted to scare us.

Fear in my stomach. I can't take my eyes off the small doll that Sally is now toying with as she laughs at her prank.

"Did I get you guys? Huh?"

"Sally…"

She laughs and Mandy goes after her playfully. She drops the Skeleton Man to the floor. It tumbles and the fear grows. Heavy and thick in the back of my throat now.

I grab the doll.

"What is that?" Amanda asks.

"I found it in my room when we moved in. Isn't it creepy!" Sally said. She made a move towards it.

Like a mother with her child I quickly hid the figure away. I didn't want Sally to even lay her eyes on it. It was something dangerous.

"Rich, what…"

"I don't know what this is…"

"It's mine!" She says with a defeated and annoyed tone.

I throw my voice over hers. "But my grandfather told me never to touch it."

Chills shiver all over my skin. It pricks in tiny bumps all along it. I feel a presence in the basement with us.

The light flickers.

Sally moves back and Amanda wraps her arms around her.

"I don't know what he used it for but I know he'd be mad if we touched it."

We all say nothing. Silence between us. Suddenly Sally goes to grab it. "I'll put it back where I found it."

As her tiny hands grab for the manmade stitching, the light above us bursts. Glass and electricity shoot about the room. A haunting glow buzzes from the fuse and many faces begin to twist about.

Sally screams and grabs me by the waist. Amanda moves close to. We fall to the floor as the fear shocks us all.

Someone with angst in his heart moves towards us. In the pitch dark blackness we see nothing. We only feel one another as we shake with paranoia. All three of us hear his breathing. Feel as he steps closer to us.

Then we see his face.

Mangled and rotted.

Amanda screams and runs. She trips over herself as she makes her way up the stairs. The window blasts open, more glass shattering about. A powerful gale moves through the room.

The haunted ghost lingers and burns his glare at us.

I grab Sally and we make our way up the wooden exit.

The man moves an arm at us just as we make our steps onto the structure to escape.

Upstairs the party is in chaos.

Amanda already made her dramatic entrance and everyone is screaming to figure out what's happening. My mother demands we tell her what happen as we enter the kitchen.

Sally is pale with fear. She says nothing.

I dropped the Skeleton Man as Sally made a grab for me.

"Mom, I don't know…"

And again, as if he was playing with his timing and taking cues from me, the lights flickered. One by one the bulbs exploded. The party goers were thrown into panic and they made a mad dash towards the various doors. Punch and food were tossed to the floor. It too began to tremble. As the frenzied crowd began to exit the walls began to ooze. Water or slime or wax you could call it, started to melt down the walls. It covered the people in it's slop. They choked on it. The slipped and tumbled over themselves on it.

Spiders and flies poured from the vents of the house. A woman screamed so loud I felt my ears were going to pop.

The spiders were crawling all about her.

My mother was grabbing Sally and trying to make her way to the front exit.

My father was trying to calm people. Help them exit.

The fire in the front room was dead. In it's place, fog and rancid smell. Toxic odor that made people gag. Mr. Simmons was throwing up all over the couch. My dad made his way into the room as I tried to look away. The sound of further disgust was heard. The smell itself overpowering.

I saw as my mom was screaming for me to leave. Her and Sally were just at the front door.

A man and wife collapsed at the foot of the stairs.

As I tried to move to help them I caught it. The light glistening from the approaching crimson.

A sea of blood poured down from the second floor. It drowned the two fainted and knocked over the exited people. My mother was knocked down and out of the house. Her hand was out stretched towards me.

The bloody river was helping clean out the remaining unlucky who were caught inside. I try to gain composure. To ignore my fear and find my father.

I feel his hand on my back.

"Let's get the fuck out of here."

And that's that.

I give into the fear and let the adrenaline move my legs. The scarlet liquid rushes onto my sneakers as I step over the unconscious bodies.

Sally and my mom are already getting into the car as people run a menace all down the street. The houses are all alive now with noise and lights. Sirens are heard in the distance. So many wails and screams are heard. Both in confusion and utter fear. My dad screams for my attention.

With the fear now all across my heart I no longer feel the house or it's eyes. I only feel the need to get into the car.

I look at the darkness as my dad steps on the gas. Blood and puke drenched, we all sit in quiet, dead silence. Nothing is felt but confusion, relief, fear, sorrow, and angst.

All from the house.

All from a place unknown.

I only look down at my shoes as my dad drives along the road. We don't stop for hours.

-END-

TINY LITTLE FINGERS

In tiny little boxes, that's how they appear. After the parents begin to worry when their child is no longer safe in their bed. The fear creeps on their brow as they pull the crimson lace.

Tiny white boxes house sweet horrors. Painful clues that point to their tortured spawn. Mom and dad tossed into chaos. Panic and anger. Deep sorrow and confusion. A royal flush of emotion.

Tiny little fingers in tiny white boxes.

Soon the house is a buzz with words, in angst, and in sadness, phone calls to police. Information tossed aside like valuable garbage.

First mistake.

They should take more caution. Hold their dear child's finger longer. Read out the message on it's skin.

No.

They leave it to the cops. The big heads with badges and to them, the power to stop him. Their child cries in the hollows of his home. He wants to be caught to loose the game he begun many months ago.

Six children dead and gone. Their bones laid to unjustified rest. Tears echo down parents faces. Ignorant eyes mourn for answers they may never receive.

But he wants to loose. Death's Cold Right Hand.

The newspaper bled his horror. Pages blazed his gory and words of mass hysteria spoke to masses. Who was this monster?

Death's unforgiving hand.
He found them.

The Moellers.

Pete and Martina Moeller.

Daughter Marle.

She was pure.

Skin like porcelain. It made the beast salivate. He could taste her. His devilish desires burning in his eyes, he watched and learned all about his prey.

Watched them deeply. Madly he peeled away their security and got as close to the sun as his perverted wax wings could carry. He snatches her. Quickly and coolie.

At the park as her nanny Rosie talked to Beth and Blair. All three took no notice. She came for the candy. He smiled that monster smile and she was his. The monster had Marle.

And soon there came a package. The tiny white box. At exactly three in the morning. Burned off at one end, the knock at the door only added to it's haunted arrival. Martina answered the door. Pete with the bat close behind. She fainted at it's sight. Red glowing ribbon. Pete ran into the cold and darkened street.

The beast was off to sleep in his bed. Freshly cleaned wounds on his back weep as the stars carry him to sleep. Peter now thrown into a revenge wakened state. He wanted the beast dead.

There wasn't time. The frantic hero ignored his wife as she laid in the open doorway. He grabbed the box and as he tried to fight the fear now trembling his hands, he opened it.

Marle's soft and elegantly mutilated pinky fell to the floor. Martina began to stir, Peter now weeping. He reached for the finger and knew he'd have to fight the urge to vomit.

His eyes traced the tender curves of the skin. No markings, no words, nothing. No answers. Pete dropped the tortured object. Then he saw the ribbon.

Elegant words written along it's seductive surface. He untied the perfectly tied bow just as Martina rose to her feet. She muttered softly to the night.

Peter tried to read the words but the letters were all jumbled. None of it made sense. Just letters thrown together. The fear was pressing against the roof of his head. Tensing up. More questions when all he desperately wanted were answers. Martina mentions phoning the police.

The shaken hero doesn't know what to do. He gets some water. The two talk. The house alive with emotion. The rest of the world asleep. Young at heart now in their unparalleled fear, they talk for hours. Dawn ready to break, they decide to wait. To try and figure out the message on the ribbon.

Peter convinces her of the danger of giving the entire case to the police. To be willing to be put out of the loop. To turn over all information to the men in badges with no chance to try and solve it on their own merits.

She cries more tears and says the pain her stomach won't stop. Peter soothes her. She falls asleep in is arms. His eyes press as he blankly stares at the window. The street outside slowly coming into light. The weight of all these sudden dark moments gets to him. He falls asleep.

The day is a blur of sounds and the routine. He goes to work. Peter not having the guts to call off during busy season. Martina works when she wants to. She's the lead boss. Pete doesn't recall her calling in or even moving from the couch.

That's where she was when he came home from work. Curled up in a fetal position. Heavy breathing. The beast is readying another gift. Metal on flesh. Tied with a ribbon. He cleans himself.

Peter gets food fro the fridge. A cup of Jell-O and an apple. His first meal. It's bitter against his psyche. It feels forced.

"You gotta eat."
"Where is she?"
He winces. "Please...."
It's all the same. Him caressing her, trying to make her relax. To just think about something else. But it felt hypocritical. Like he wanted to say it to himself. All he saw was her face. Blood and her beautiful smile. Tears well up but never fall.

Hours pass, each one like a whip on their backs. it was slowed. time. No noise. Just the two of them. Martina didn't start to move until ten at night. Pete moved about the house but in quiet shifts. He changed, and watched the photo of his first dog hung in his bathroom.

He came downstairs and watched Tina breathing. Smiling to himself if not to ease the pain. Now night was a blanket and the beast was stirring.

He crept out of his home and took a stroll. Visited the park and made a commotion in the stillness of the outside. Alone and plotting.

85

Continued on his way, slithering about in the shadows.

Peter and Martina spoke on one word moments.
They ate.
Crying into their food.
They fucked.
If not to pass the time.
They felt like monsters.
Not knowing what to do. When either of them closed their eyes they saw her face. It was as still as a photo. Neither of them planned on it. They say the one followed the other, but together they crept up to Marle's room.

Her scent. Soft and sweet. Martina collapsed in her bed. Hues of pink brightened their sorrow. Pete sat at her feet.
Quiet and stillness.
No sound of life at all.
A home.
Waiting for another terrible clue.

In a flash the real monster made his way to their home. Each step a sort of rhythmic death stomp. He held his breath. The usually sane police. Commotion and chaos.

But still the house was quiet, another model home in the row and others like it. Street lights painted out the hollow feeling of the group of housing. He delivered the package but made only one knock before quickly moving into the nights cover.

He felt pain. A sort of horrid destruction. A home a buzz with lights ringing out in the night, trailing as haunting all day. He wanted chaos. His fangs wet with it. Justice felt close. A climax building on his crooked brow. He never made it to clue three.
Police had dogs.
He forced to stay the price, always felt the cage build. Every foiled game left the hole bigger. The blood scented rooms pained him more than anything.
Torture is his lust.
Death, his curse.

The two souls awake, time and the space around them but a dream. Soaked feeling. Pete made coffee. Drank a shot or two of vodka. Marty drank from the bottle. He remembered the knock.

She says it was like a nightmare. In a painful silence they make their way to the door. So much tension on their minds. The box lay just outside.

Lavender.
Both in scent and color.
Tears build but never fall.
Another finger.

In a sickeningly sincere way Marty holds and caresses it. She looks off into the living room. No words said. Peter looks at the ribbon.

"M RR R"

Too many other thoughts. Trying not to scream. Holding back vomit and sorrow. Wanting another shot. Her face. Screaming in the distance. Quiet noises in his home. He can't piece it together. He folds and unfolds the smooth ribbon in his hands. The letters dance on his brain. "M. R. R. R." he says to the night.

Marty only seems distantly interested. Far yet close enough to understand that her husband spoke. She too only saw her face. "M. R. R. R." he says again. This time directly to his love. Her eyes wet with pain and anger. She grabs the ribbon.

Peter says it again. "M. R. R. R."
Marty never drops the index clue.
"Miner."
Her voice hollow and cold.
"Mirror?" Peter asks.

She drops the ribbon and starts to pace. Alone in her fleeting emotions. Hearing her response repeat to himself a few of his previous thoughts dissipate. He hears it clear as day.

"Mirror."

In a dull and almost robotic motion he retrieves the first ribbon from his pocket. Two clues. Two nights of gruesome reality. Almost asking for figments of falsehood. For this to be over and done. The other ribbon starts to burn. Peter goes to the washroom. Blood on his hands. He turns on the faucet. He takes the first ribbon. Mangled letters seem to bleed. The reflection spins in the bright fluorescents.

"Marle Moeller Lives"

Someone screams it. It whispers to his left. She was alone. He knew it, or should have all along. His breath is caught in his lungs, his revelation pressing onto his thoughts. Two nights, and she was alive. The ribbon said so. Maybe it was crazy. He felt like he might be. But the cops normally made a loud ruckus. A commotion.

Maybe this was a game. A sick and twisted designer murder. he laughs to himself. It echoes. Marle is alive. And each night he'd get closer. Hell, he felt that if his childhood taught him anything, it was cheaters always win.

He'd cheat .
He'd get Marle back.

Running frantically he shakes Marty from her frazzled rut. She drops the fingers, goes to grab it but he stops her. Peter kisses her. Martina sheds a tear. "She's alive." Suddenly her face brightens.

The emotion leaking onto her lips and turning out a wonderful smile. One that throws them into a passion. Joy in an ocean of sorrow. They had to hold this hope. Had to beat this monster and get Marle back.

The two parents only wished it was their fingers they were loosing. Moonlight kisses and hope soaked tears. Liquor softens away ache. They overwhelm themselves with this new emotion. This electricity.

It was like Marle had returned. Like the three of them now sat and laughed for the joy of reuniting. Her pain over now. Mutilation be damned.

They would truly cherish her.
Love her close.
They felt that underlying love.
Once Marle returned, never again.
More care.
More love.
Slow down and enjoy life's elegant flowers.
Time off work.

Love Marle.

Love one another.

The stars painted away into soft dawn light. Like before Marle lay in Pete's lap. The warmth of their bright future. It felt cool and refreshing. A beautiful sound sleep.

He moves now in the burning sun. Darkness no longer to hide him. A monster in mans skin. To passersby nothing more then a common man. No concern to them. Even though his hands were now stained a soft and tortured hue of pink.

No soap nor chemicals could get rid of it. It burned.

The beast stops at the park.

Children move about and play with no fear. Parents, guardians and paid help only watch now as they live out a many dozen fantasies. their glorious cries of pure happiness stings against his ears.

Yet he feels nothing else. Little more then impending end. He quenched for it so. Day and night before hand. Each death hurt too. And yet.

He stood now at the park. Clue in pocket. Thumb caressing the lace. Marle was alive. Her torture so great and powerful, it tickled the monster. Eased the pain of the now. Each scream that burned in memory beautiful and delicious to recall. Wetting his teeth with a lust for more. He moves.

No desire to remain in such sunlight. It was too much. He needed the solace of his quiet home. With each step he grew more impatient to return to Marle.

If this was to end then he would enjoy the last minutes with this sweet angel. The house still as quiet as ever. Death and sorrow caught in the reflection of the dying sunlight. Wind so haunting he felt a need to run.

These were the hero's. The right to his wicked wrongs. It chilled his bones to be near this place. To dwell was to cause great damage to his psyche. He drops the box and runs. Not looking back. The beast feels fear.

A sickly sweet and unsuspected paranoia. Fear and the end so close. His heart roared in his chest. Only the burns to the captured angels skin could make fear cease.

Marty awoke to Pete kicking the door. Daylight a fading thing.

Time was such a blue now. they felt pulled from reality. Lost in a chaos with hope so close it made time feel insignificant. Pete held the box in his hand. Door open.

A neighbor across the street peering in. Marty give her a wave and closes the door. Pete ways a few angered words to the sudden quiet.

"We missed the delivery."

She tries to coax him. it seems that her words do nothing but feed his new found doubt.

"I gotta stay awake. Gotta watch him make the drop off. Kill the fucking bastard."

She gives him reason. They could sleep in shifts. Try and catch him together. Peter can't grasp full responsibility.

"It's as much my fault as it is yours." He scoffs.

They speak in cold and void tones. Sentencing without much thought or emotion. Tension now winding between them. He holds a card now. The box in pieces in the entry way. Marle's finger lay forgotten. She grabs it. Places on the vanity mirror. In the foggy emotion and stillness she moves to the kitchen. Peter inspects a small card.

Red in color.
White text.
"LOOK INTO THE PAST"

He clicks his teeth. Martina returning with a bag of clues. Placed on ice. Three little fingers.

Burned. Cut. Peeled.

Each crying Marle's bitter cries. Marty catches the vomit in her throat. Tiny fingers of her daughter.

"What time did you drop off Marle at Rosie's?"

"What?"

Caught off guard. He asks again. Too many tangled thoughts. Memories all caught together. When did he too last see his angel?

Recount the steps and again the tension winds. Rosie requested she watch her over at her place, as she was without a car and could only travel by foot. The memory felt false. Was that this week? Or did Rosie stop by? Marty often left after Pete. Once or a dozen times before she left before Rosie even arrived.

Chills along her back.

No, she dropped her off at Rosie's. She recalls Marle pointing at a boy near the park. Lucas from her class. Or was it a girl? Marty feels weak. More uneasy emotions leak out. Peter feeling more secure in his recollection of the pat few days. Doubt with every moment Marty spoke.

Maybe he did so to ease the now heavy guilt. Not sure but still so the two spoke in angst. Marty defending her spoken fragments Pete worked more hours. Marty often came home late.

The revelation and inspection of the clue only poured away into a fight left behind the curtain. Waiting on both ends for the moment of lights.

Now this was about them.

Each trying to press away the sorrow and wave of emotions. They were like children. Both afraid of the reality that they were both horrible parents.

They failed to protect Marle.

Both of them.

So caught up in themselves and the lives they portrayed to an audience of no one. A climax was reached. Pete slamming his fist in the wall. Anger so pure it burned like ruby.

They embraced.

For they knew that this did them no good. No need to spread the infection of hate. Fuel the anger. They ate in the bitter quiet. Sun fading off and night now a brilliant portrait of life.

Pete watched the window.

Marty slept. They switch. Marty pacing about the house. So painfully dull with not a noise to stir the emotion.

She makes her way to her bedroom and peers from the top window. The street is still.

As the fresh morning turns to high afternoon, Marty grows more anxious. The night was over. She can't remember when the stars had faded.

Looking out to the people on the street and time suddenly felt cruel. cold and unforgiving. She had no grasp on it. Once feeling so slow she could count the seconds, now suddenly burning away. it was too much. This house was becoming her prison. A lust to escape it continues seeps through.

Maybe a nice lunch at her favorite café might ease all of this raw emotion. Peter is showering. The sound of the running water makes the lust pulse. She grits her teeth.

91

Pen on post-it, she scribbles a note to her husband. chills creep up her back as the writing recalls the heartless clues.

'Had to get out. Be right back.'

All around her the world is alive. People move about their day with no knowledge of the terrible things Marty is enduring.

She walks in a quiet. conversation and street noise are the back drop. She misses Marle. Her heart aches. Too much to just ignore. Café is full. Jazz music on full blast. Life is a buzz. Too much too soon.

Martina coughs.

Peter steps into stale air.

Quiet silence now engulfed their home. A powerful odor of noise that before felt bearable. Time made it harder. Cleans up and goes down the stairs. A note on the vanity. No seats for Marty to sit. Pete feels a hazy anger. It blooms but withers.

He understands.

She eats quietly outside in the open air. Out on the patio it was easier to not feel surrounded. As enclosed as before. Now she felt paranoid. Sickeningly crazy because she had a curiosity about her. Peter eats too in silence. Ham and cheese in the sunlight. No noise. Yet they hear her playing.

When she enters the house she sees Pete asleep, fetal position. She goes upstairs. In the high light of the midday she has a moment. Just outside Marle's room. Her being runs past. Marty grabs her chest. Joy and pain. She changes her clothes. No need to shower. Puts on comfortable clothing. Wants to wake Pete. Tell him to give up and turn in. Give the police a call and let them win the game.

She was done. Tired. Nothing left but sorrow and anger. At herself. Failure. As she steps down the stairs Pete wakes. he looks at her as she crosses the threshold to the living room.

They stare.

One can cut the silence. She tries to smile but the weight of the issue on her mind was too much. Peter could tell. Something was off. Off even for a situation as grim as this.

"You alright?"

She nods. Moves to the couch. They sit at opposite ends.

"Sorry I fell asleep."

"Sorry I had to get out."

They smile. Hearts beat in a haunted unison in the quiet.

"You sure your alright?"
She bites her lip. He waits.
"I think we should call the police."

She says it with conviction. Quiet. Read. Sudden rush of thoughts and Peter's in a flurry. Not sure what to say.

three days of waiting and playing it safe. Day four. Day fucking four. He out bursts.

"Now? Now you want to get them involved?"
She puts up a fight. She now standing as she feels useless in her own daughter's life. Takes it out on him. Peter argues they agreed to wait it out. He read the headlines. He knew this guy was sick. But he wanted to get Marle back. Not leave it to a cop.

"Please. They can get search dogs."
Anger
Marty wants quick justice.
At least to him.
He can see a future with Marle ending in body bags. Not going to happen. the clues. It was a game. He was going to cheat and win if it meant he too would die.

She weeps.
Only briefly.
Now unsure.

The two don't mean to argue. But still the words pour. The soul now plots. Never made it this far. He was wet with anticipation. Made him shiver. Marle weeps as he enjoys the setting sum. So much work left to do.

The weight of the end now feeling so close that the beast's own heart raced.

Fear too crept in.

In a quiet key. Off behind the melody of the joy. The game was being played. It made him joyful so. Argument over. They stand in a hushed stillness. Neither know what to say.

They agree to wait this one more night. To try and catch him in the act of delivering the note. Pete would surprise him from the bushes just outside their house.

But still Marty knew not of the future. Would this work? Would Marle live and truly they'd be together again? A new hope. That's what Peter's sudden kiss brought. With it his trust. Passion. She smiled.

"I'm going to cook you dinner."

He's off to the kitchen.

Martina goes to the closet. To recount memories. to think of future ones to come. Marle is alive here. In photos and old items long forgotten. All is a little too heavy to bare but Marty endures and is happy as she dives into the past. Pete is moving quickly.

Time to him but fleeting background. Nothing to concern with. He was alive on the moon and sun. And the monster's clues. Turns the radio on. One of his favorite songs. He dances as he creates his wife's meal. More photos.

The beast stirs from his work. Her smile. To taste a moment of silence. His victim now asleep from pain. With his eyes closed he lets the sound of after shock set in. A soft buzz. Harmony in peace.

She places her fingers on the photo of Marle in ballet. Tears well. Peter enters with joy on his weakened heart. They dance.

Laugh in the drowning sea of unease. The beast too dances on his wicked and cruel actions. The tormented future and end. The meal is wonderful even though the underlying thoughts keep them grounded. They feel guilty but try to move past it.

Guilt will only add weight to all this. So they drink some wine as they finish their late dinner. Setting sun and night moves love between them. Stars slowly fading in. Marty washes the dishes as Pete takes a moment to collect himself.

He stares out the window. Not so much alive as it was before but still a reminder that their pain meant so little. Great as it was, only to them. Moving out into the air the beast starts to prepare himself. A long night and day ahead. so much work left to do.

The girl sleeps now.

Peter takes in all he can in the withering day light. As Marty comes from behind, a warm embrace, he notices.

The mail box is full.

Little red flag up.

Shivers rise up as he moves away from his love. Cold felt within her. His eyes unblinking. The door is flung open and the frigid air of the outside burst in. Martina calls out but our hero moves so fast her words fall to the floor.

Tiny white box.

Red lace.

Left in the mailbox.

His teeth clench and he wants to scream. when did he leave this one? Who was to blame for it's delivery going unnoticed? All the thoughts catching on his brain and he runs inside. Marty noticing the box and her heart races. Another finger left to point the way to the finish line. It's as cold as ice in Martina's hands.

A photo now.

No words on lace.

Box lines with a scene of a sun lit playground void of human life. Trees close in above. Peter feel the connection close, on his tongue but vague and distant.

"Locust Park."

She says it and it clicks. The park. Rosie takes her to. Peter brought her there himself only once. It pains him to think of the times he rejected to go. He's unsure of his own daughter's talent or skill. Can she ride a bike? Throw a ball? Who was Marlene to him? Was he even an important figure to his daughter? Did Rosie hold more weight? Marty holds back tears and ignores the blame that requires. it's owner. She is sure it's her fault, but she knew too not to bring it up.

No need to fight. Not now. When both hearts were already defeated. Neither knowing what to do. Visit the park? Would he be there. Would he use the absence in the house to deliver more torture. Suddenly they spin their fears. To the empty and haunted home the two lovers talk and let out all they wish not to happen.

Their deep and frigid paranoia. Would Marle even still be alive?

"I'll go to the park."

Marty disagrees.

95

"I don't want to be alone in this house."
Silence.
"What would he do to me?"
Silence. Deadly.
"I don't know."
Both unsure of their next move. Too many questions demanding the solution. Should they go together? What if Marle was alive…dead? Peter kisses her.
"I have to go."
She says nothing.
It's all in her eyes.
Tears unfallen.
"Wait for him to show….something…."
A weak smile
"Go."
Another kiss.

He pulls her into the kitchen. Marty stands at the doorway. Pete moves about. Locking the back door and the windows. Checking out the night and dark outside one last time. Opening a drawer. Butcher knife.

"Take it."
Fear of death.
Dying alone.
Twister of fear.
Swept away by one kiss. Peter leaves. Marty stares out the open door. For only a moment she swears she can hear her daughter call to her father.
In the dying moon the monster drinks. For the first time in months. Painful bitter liquor mixed with even stronger memories. the man he was before.
Another shot.
Quiet.
Except for her whimpers.
He smiles and his fangs catch the starlight. Twinkle in the glass of the whiskey. Shot slams down. This had been fun. Stalking his prey. Luring them close. Taking their clues. Their…first.

He laughs. Another shot. How many spoiled games had he begun and had to finish. The whiskey speaks to him. Maybe he did enjoy taking life. Being in total control of fate. Of someone's very breath. He felt no control in his life. Divorce. Settlement. Court. Prison time. Too much bitter angst.

No.
He had control now.
She cries for someone.
The name a bloody lipped mess.
He tries to stand and his world spins about.
Liquor spilling on the carpet. Death was a rush in itself. Maybe he could bring death and play a game. Lips to glass and it scorches his throat. So disgustingly sweet. It was his puzzle. His game. A new clue is tormented into existence. A time limit. Death set to an appointment. How sickeningly ironic.
More liquor. Monster now overjoyed with his cruel endeavor. He howls to the wails of the girl. He licks her tears. Finishes the bottle. As he preps the final clue his world grows heavy. Turning to milky gray. Fuzzy now and he climbs upstairs.

Mouth dry from booze he makes it to the couch. Collapses. It dreams of future torture. Of escape. The liquor hid the notion of fear but now it was unimportant. No need for being caught. He'd run. Still achieve death.

It dreams of freedom and death. Blood soaked fantasy and the beast sleeps. In the deserted park Peter feels tormented.
"Was this where he grabbed you?" He says to the phantom.
He sheds a tear.
A sort of cold rushes over.

He strolls the park and false memories press. Fragments of hope. One day he'd bring her back here. No. A better park. He'd play with her all day. He smiles and he winces. He should have made the effort before. Taken the time. Under fading stars he feels guilty. Utterly guilty.
The silence of the playground pains him as well. He finds a middle ground. An under shrub. The beast won't show tonight. He can feel it in his gut. But he needed rest. If not to skip ahead in time. To reach Marle and the night faster.

Peter counts the stars. Lulls himself to a harsh and cold sleep. Sings himself a quiet lullaby. Like he should have done to Marle. How so much now he pained to hold her again. To tell her it'd all be okay.

The stars fade.

Peter falls asleep.

Children play in the comfortable sun. Laughter soaks through the air and wakes Peter. Not sure no one saw him, clear. Pete moved like a ghost. He observed the park. Became the beast. Invisible, he saw the moms and nannies. Kids playing with little more then sugar and imagination.

Peter sees a phantom. Make play too. She laughs amongst the others. He thirsts and hungers. First time in days. Holding still the waning guilt he goes for a coffee and donut.

Buys two. One for him. One for Marle. A pink sprinkled chocolate. Her favorite. If he can recall the few time he spent with her. More guilt. He calls Marty. She's mute. Dull. He says he's going to walk the perimeter of the park.

Plots how now he'll stalk this sick bastard. He's unsure his wife's even listening. Fear now getting to her. She says little. sound of water boiling. Loud tea kettle and she leaves without an I love you.

"Love you too." he says to the dial tone.

He spends the rest of the daylight watching for the monster. anyone or anything he thought was suspicious. With angered eyes he watches. Paces the park. Marks the perimeter. Inspects every face that enters the now hollow grounds.

Ground zero.

Heart still racing, never slowing. In the resting dusk he finds a camp site for the late. back in the forgotten bushes he waits for stars.

One more night.

Day five.

One whole hand now offered up in insight. Awful mess. Painful tragedy. the sunset takes too long. Pete hums to pass the time.

The monstrosity is a foot. Moving in soft sun light. He has so much left to do. Clue in claw he makes his way to the home. Amongst the sea of life. Another face in the crowd. an everyday man, with a tiny box tucked in his pocket.

Soon thrown into a mailbox. As the metal of the container snaps shut he runs. a shock of quick fear propels him. Must grab Marle. Heat on his back and he's sprinting. Time meant more now then ever. Panting like the animal within, he reached his home. So much left to do. He prepared for the night. Fear and doubt hung above. Soft tears in the back track. A long night ahead.

Unison
The beast stirs.
Hero awakes.
Pale moon just as before.
A mother longs for tomorrow.
Looks out into the stars. Eyes caught in a gaze. Time shifts. Peter now standing. Beast working hard. Aware of the minutes slowly passing. Moon beating down. Shovel to earth and he works even harder. Marty can't recall the day. More false memories burn. Did she sleep?
Chamomile lips.
Peter walks towards the noise. Monstrous breathing. So haunting. She sleeps. Unaware. Fate clicks forward. The hero now within eye shot of our poor villain trying to hide the prize away. Throwing dirt into the stars bright twinkle.

Marle lay near. He's atop the killer. Rage pouring over. Hands on throat. Knuckles to bone. Again, again. Powerful angst forms in the night air. She was to the mailbox. Almost crushes the box. More cutting of flesh in madness.

Two animals in the night.
He fights for love.
He fights for life.
Lace falls. She reads;
"DUSK."

Fingers press and she's now in a chaos. She tries to reach her husband. Teeth clench. More skin peeling. He's got him. Blood shines and falls. Joy. Anger. Fear. All emotion cascades over.
No answer. She worries. More chaos. Fear gaining weight. She takes a moment. As do the two beasts. They glare at one another. Peter grabs at the clean air. So does the monster.
Gravitation in a fury moves and the two fight again. Claws and bones move. Pain. Shatter the weaker. More pain. She makes a move of

desperation. A sort of guilt sweeps over. Sirens breathe to life. Monsters caught in their struggle.

Keep the fire burning. She weeps.

Our heroine cries.

Not sure of the future.

But Marle stirs. Alert. Pete gains his light.

Overcomes the beast.

Just as he smashes the skull, red and blue and that horrible pitch of sound.

He collects himself. Marle sits. Quiet. The police draw closer. Beast slain.

"Daddy?"

They embrace. As the flashing lights out., there are tears of joy and sorrow. Moonlight now covering the stars. Engulfing the scene of fear. A scene of faith. Of conquering the demons within. Marty feels it too. The love of family. A warmth that carries across the distance.

-END-

A LOVE STORY

The sun was hanging powerfully high, strung up on a brilliantly bright hope of romance promised. Air swept through the small caravan, wrapping our fate crossed lovers in a warm summer bliss. Air so sweet it melted on Mandy's heart strings. Run away. Typical, if not beautifully tragic. Beautiful in all aspects.

Amanda Paige was the teen dream. Looks that had all the boys at South Bend taking notice. Right through Senior year. Even on Graduation day, she was the brilliant diamond in a sea of glass crystals. Her brains were parent's secret wishes. The ones they hid through their teeth when disappointing grades lined report cards. She had it all.

'And you're throwing it all away!' her disappointed mother had said.

Two weeks ago.

It had been a month since she was valedictorian. Giving her final speech to a crowd of admirers.

A month and three weeks since her and Tony Bennett decided to get married.

Tony's hand shifts the gear nervously. It shakes about; their car bouncing recklessly on the mountain roads.

More trees.

Tall pine trees that made the blowing wind fresh.

Not too many clouds.

Azure blue skies.

Amazing hope for a better tomorrow.

Mandy's father owned a large pharmaceutical company. They specialized in various treatment for everyday aches and pains. Her mother ran most of the advertising half of the business. That is to say, both parents were very wealthy and well respected in their community.

Tony's parents? They too ran a business. A pharmaceutical one. Amanda's parent's biggest rivals. Every one of Mr. Paige's pills had an exact, if not better, twin pill that was produced by FamilyFirst Medicine.

And the insignificant war that started with Health Tru Pharmaceuticals slandering their rivals as thieves to major media groups was now ending in outlandish and opera like court battles. Everyone was under a microscope as inside secrets were being thrown about.

This is how our dear lovers first met.

Amanda looks out at the scenery for more then haunting pine wood.

She sees rocky cliff sides. Large brown rocks dancing outward at her. Telling a story of years past.

101

She folds her hands.

Tony can't take his eyes off the road. This kind of driving made him nervous. The mountain roads were unforgiving. Twisting up and suddenly curving; dropping down into another deadly curve.

His heart beat with anticipation. Anticipation and love.

He smiles.

In the second trial over some assault on the street between two of their respective parent's team members. That's what it was. A battle between two ruthless parties. During the court room drama, Tony was asked to take the stand.

He was witness to his own sides anger issues. The man in question was a Randall Cliff. Cliff burst out at a Christmas Party and struck Tony's now ex-girlfriend.

The young blonde pressed charges.

She wasn't there that day.

Amanda watched as Tony spoke of the night when Mr. Cliff got too aggressive. He was even dressed as Santa Claus.

Amanda sees a bird high above in the sky sea.

Wings spread out.

She thinks on another issue. One not involving her putting a hold on school.

Tony's age.

He was twenty three.

Our sweet miss pulls on her red skirt. The pigeon makes a call before disappearing. The road shakes them.

He was a full five years older then she was. Sometimes she would pull at the thought of that being too old.

That maybe he was too much for her. Had seen so much more. Had done five years worth of living before she was even a glimmer.

Radio statics out.
Tony looks over.
They catch eyes.
Like they did in that courtroom almost a year ago.

A powerful gaze that spoke of unsaid emotion.
A lust to seek out more. To answer the questions of their own

beating hearts.

She smiles.
Her fingers on his.
His eyes back on the road.
The thought of ages snaps.
Drifts away.
Cars zip past to their left. Making them nervous one might veer into them.
They had to run away.

Take the long drive to Tony's old roommate's. A little place he called a 'safe haven' from their folks.
Back in Oregon, they could never be together.
Not when their parents wanted the other dead. Or too busy tearing at one another's throat to see that they were in love.

Her father struck her when she told him.
Her hand rubs the soft memory sensation that soothes on her cheek.
Mr. Paige had never done that before but when she came out and told him she was to marry Tony, he let it all out. In one swift motion he let his emotion come full force.
A phantom tear falls down.

Tony didn't tell his folks.
Doesn't speak to them.
They used to not care he lived in their old summer home but once he made his many testimonies against his own family, he was out.
Been out on his own every day after that.

Washington was a chance to start fresh for both of them. He truly felt love in his heart for Amanda.
She was mature beyond her years. So much more to the beautiful girl then anyone could know. He was first to admit that she might be too good for him.
Another smile.
The road opens.

More traffic.

His eyes look about the crazy movement of vehicles.

Amanda sings for a moment with the music on the radio. Quiet but sweet like honey.

It wraps a beat of love around Tony.

"I love you."
"I know."

They laugh.

They were inseparable the moment the two met in that busy court. People crossing all around.

His eyes on hers.

They spoke briefly.

Both too weak too speak. A true love unbroken.

Moments swept past.

Candle light love and romance, sugar sweet. Each day and every night that they spent in each others company burned in passion. So powerful. Like the leading sun.

The other cars move along like the chained up memories of secret bliss. Under painted stars he told her he truly felt for her.

She cried.

The feeling was returned.

Stars sparkled.

Tony's fierce features were the fatal attraction. She was his once she saw his raw beauty. His grit. Then he spoke and to her young heart it was like poetry.

Her friends were jealous. He was like a phantom wish; a twilight lover that came to her on her childish dreams of love.

That's why she couldn't give this up.

It felt like nothing she had ever experienced.

An animal love and a fiery lust that tugged on every ounce of her being.

The wind catches her hair in the up draft.

She pulls it back.

Tony thinks back as a red car moves in front of him.

It looked like the one she left behind.

He thinks back to when he found out her age.

She was only seventeen.

Jaw to the floor he felt foolish. Totally and utterly fooled. Almost disgusted with himself for having had eyes for someone younger then he.

But she pursued. She called him. There was something there. Something sweet and almost like fate. He never believed in such a thing. Not before now. Love and that emotion were just ideas he spoke of amongst his friends. He knew lust before. Before an unparalleled love that out powered those carnal desires.

Driving along roads unknown and new he felt like he was doing the right thing. Driving along fate's invisible line.

Edgar lived in Olympia. A small town that had lots of promise.

Amanda wanted to be a teacher. There was a good school located there. Another shimmer of hope.

The two kept driving.

They had been doing this tango of dropping it all; leaving it all behind for two weeks.

Uncertain. Afraid. In love. Out of options. A need for something new. A get away from it all.

They danced with the fates. Finally deciding that they would take Edgar's generous offer of free room and board with out question.

She hummed the new tune that came to life on the speakers.

The scenery is a little different here and there. More tall and haunting woods, but different plant life all the same. Wild carves of mountains. It all changed a bit.

Almost became ugly in some respects.

Tony tried to think of the days ahead.

The life he was overjoyed to be sharing with his scarlet hearted angel.

A car cuts them off.

His fists punch the wheel.
"Asshole."
Se caresses his leg.
He smiles at her.
"We're almost there."

Almost free. She could swear she felt the weight of her parents and their unnecessary aggression and disappointment fading off. Turning into dust.

She puts her hand out the open window.
Curling and swimming along the drafts of air, she moves her arm like a snake.
Every moment that passed, each car jetting away from them was another instant that shed doubt. It took these tiny weights away from them.

Amanda had fallen in love before. Only once.

Leonardo Valmont.
Her dear Leo.

They met when they were in preschool. Two kids with innocence in their hearts. They grew up together. Spent the summers exploring the world around them. Two kindred souls carving out a beautiful existence.

Clouds roll in.
Only a small group of them
Soft.
She pulls her hand back into the car.

Leo died five years before.
Car accident.
The newspaper clippings and neighborhood gossip swarm inside her head. A high buzz of backwater memories that almost sting. She tries to flicker them away.
She remember how Leo's dark blues eyes spoke to her every heart string.
A thought presses on.
The same gaze burned now in Tony's eyes.

It was more powerful. More entrancing. She found the same deep passion in his eyes. Tears well up but never fall. Moments of shallow sorrow and happiness.

No more clouds.
Just pure azure sky.

As they continue to drive along they see more of their new home. T pulls up over the dominating landscape. Massive structures and beautiful waters. More life drifts in with the wind. Hope sings over the loud radio. The two speak of a better tomorrow.

"Edgar's place is huge. His parents left it to him in their will. Died last year. It's right near town."

She smiles. "Good. I was afraid we'd be closed off from the world. It's what I heard about the towns up here."

Tony laughs a low chuckle. "No. I need to be near a bar. A good one, with live music." he laughs again. "No way I'm living in the boonies."

"We can't escape our parents. They do business all over the country."

"So? We'll never fully escape less we skip the US. It's like trying to escape McDonald's or coca Cola. Hell, we'd have better luck with that. Our folks cure people remember?"

She recants, "Dozens of donations to third world countries." She breathes deep.

Tony agrees. "There's always a market for that."

Hope starts to trickle away. Amanda knows what he's saying is true. Her father prides himself with his larges sales numbers and variety of medical advances. She assumes Tony's father is the same. Dear Mandy's never met him. Never will.

Her eyes look out to the small image of her new home. It's gaining ground and her heart's beating faster.

The music on the radio is omnipresent. It sings of melancholy things. Love lost. Seeking something to erase the pain.

They catch each other's eyes. Smiles.

"Just past that bridge."

Her eyes catch the gray rigging structure high above them. It towers over everything. The roads, the woods, even the mountains themselves. It's a beast with manmade beauty.

"Bet you can see it all up there. Every ounce of this town."

"Our town."

Amanda leans over and kisses his cheek. His morning scruff brushes lovingly rough on her lips.

Soon they'd be free. No more hurt. Nothing. Only bliss. Endless romance only fate could write. Only time could hold out so long. This would truly be forever love.

Endless.

The bridges crept closer.

The mountains curled up on either side of them.

So delicate and proud. Brown fragments grabbed at her attention.

Tony took a moment to look about him. So many cars. They didn't take notice to them. Just fragments. They cared not for their runaway hearts and bad fated love. He took this as a sign. It was meant to happen. Their chance meeting.

The ever hours of their lover. How their parents hated one another so. This crazy twist of running away from it all.

He gritted his teeth.

It only mattered to them

These two hearts.

That's why this love would last, burn eternal.

It spoke to time as a love that fought the odds and took a chance to exist. Existence that could only burn it time and fate too took a chance.

Fear struck Amanda.

For a moment her heart skipped two sequential beats. Choked up.

Would this love last?

Could it?

Love couldn't. Like all things it had to end too didn't it?

What if this was fleeting romance. Childish, star blinded bliss built on nothing but hope?

Life too ended. We all died, that was certain.

Love too must die then. This thought pulsed. Itched on Amanda's burning heart.

The sun still hung high above.
It rose up with the bridge.
She looked into Tony's eyes.
They moved along the road.
Metal open high above the car. Concrete gate away.

A deep breath.
Final and complete.
Nothing left but this.
He jumps.

Flesh meets shattering glass, tearing metal peeling back.
Amanda's skull caves in on her fleeting thoughts.
Tony's dreams splatter on his closed window pane.
Crimson paints their childish love. Their true love. Built on the now
destroyed dreams of two young hearts.

Teeth clench.
Bones crack.
Allan twitches as he looks as the car spins into traffic. The loud
noises of destruction and death pierce his bleeding ear.
Amanda silent. Her heart fading off.
Her hands on Tony's as his too fades off.
Painful shards of flesh and romance burn as their car crashes into an
oncoming truck.

Allan gets his wish as he too fades into a suicidal star dust.
Death his only hope

Dear Tony and Amanda hung up on love.
Final moments of beating romance that soon after spoke for months
on television sets. Their story of run away hope and love so powerful it killed
now bled on newspapers. Their parents bonded in this painful loss.

Two lives forever gone.
Forever in love.
Love written in the stars.

They too now dance to the twilight moon's haunting glow. Stars that shimmer on every beat.

They were love eternal.

And when lover's look into one another's eyes, if it's true; if's it's an eternal love, they too will feel this love eternal.

Signed on stars.

Amanda and Tony love.

-END-

DREAM GIRL

There was a stillness that lingered into my every pore. I stood staring deep into the well before me empty, cold. Deep within it's forgotten depths was the body of Carrie O'Brian.

For the tenth night in a row. Nothing but her and this well.

It was as if I could hear her hollow voice calling to me from within. Her name came to me with blazing frustration, a writhing pain of never knowing. Who are you and why do you haunt me so?

I awake in a cold sweat. Late for work. Another mindless day of punching numbers. The morning has a dry thickness to it. A sort of haze that feels as if I'm still dreaming. The slow and steady beating of the shower on my back. The steady calm of the pouring coffee, all of it felt so surreal.

Arriving at my office without causing too much of a commotion, I set to work fixing my technical errors. Sixes and sevens twinkled in and out of existence. I couldn't seem to focus. With each black letter, rapping of the key I heard her voice. It was there, a warm echo in the back of my subconscious. I told myself it was only my bitter loneliness getting to me. I couldn't remember the last time I went out with a woman. My life had become work, a still painting of a soulless man slaving away for nothing and no one.

My thoughts angered me so. Still I heard her soothing voice. It wrapped itself around me, caressing my inner demons and bringing me a calm. Fingers stroking the keys faster and faster. I could hear her say my name. It was soft but unmistakable. Clear through the murky waters of the dream well. Carrie sang my name, called out to me, and I drifted to her.

My mind raced with the thought of her voice, the beauty that must radiate from every waxless inch of her. The vision of her head in his hands, his fingers running through her silky hair trembled on my sanity. I was drifting to far away from my work. I shook myself clear, thoughts of her evaporating off. Then from the shadows of reality I hear her voice again.

"Allan."

A sudden wave of fear sweeps through me. Could it be I've lost my broken mind?

"Hello?"

I turn and see….what was her name? Didn't matter, she just delivered the mail to everyone in the office.

"Jumpy?"

Her dresden fingers held out a single white envelope. Reaching out I grabbed the payment from her. My face twisted itself into a nervous smile. Hoarse from awkwardness, my voice squeezed out a meager, "Thank you."

She smiled. There was an air about her. Against the current of my minds pacing she herself seemed outside my existence. A stranger I've met before. Drifted in my thoughts she walked away and over to the next cubicle. Without thinking I wheeled my chair out to see her one last time. To my surprise she turned to look back.

Scared and struck with a sudden feeling of childishness I returned to work. Again my mind became engrossed in corrections and other what not I had to become focused on.

Time had ticked away from me and soon it was time to leave. I had survived all day without too much day dreaming. The more I tried to steer myself away from these dreams of mine the more I become entangled in them. Carrie had a grip on my heartstrings. and each passing hour she strums out another somber cry.

As I made my way down the stairs I could fee a presence following suit. Reaching the bottom I heard the click of heels against the floor and there beside me stood the mailroom girl. She was a few inches shorter then I, her shallow blue eyes looking up at me with a cheerful glow.

"Hi. I know you don't know me, but I was wondering if you wouldn't mind walking home with me."

With the passing by of our coworkers and the unmistakable urge to learn more about this girl getting all a noise inside my head I agreed.

She did a sort of dance before taking my arm. The two of us walked towards the door, my mind suddenly confused with what was going on. So much static inside this head of mine that this pixie, this young girl was only a blur.

Outside in the brisk autumn air the two of us walked in a hushed crowd. People walking home from their respective places of work, the city goers doing a little shopping just before sunset. It was all a buzz, a sea of different existences all meeting and crossing for brief moments no one cared to notice.

I believe the girl had said a few things but her voice was drowned out by the sound of the street and my own racing thoughts. Where are you

Carrie and how can I find you? In this mass of people when will the two of us cross paths.

Allan

I heard her voice. It moved across my neck with the biting wind.

Allan

My eyes traced the sidewalk and up towards the mail girl. She was walking a steady pace.

"We have to cross Locust Park now. This is the part where I get scared." She drew closer to me.

Allan

"You mind?" she asked as she once again took my arm.

I forced a smile and said, "I don't" but inside I was screaming that I needed a minute.

Allan....don't forget me....

"I would never."

"What?", she asked. The two of us slowed down a little bit.

I hadn't realized that I had said anything aloud. My teeth chattered as I didn't give her a reply.

Allan...don't....please....

Shut up. My mind was suddenly a one room apartment, it's two occupants on the edge of insanity.

You can't leave me....

I won't

The mailroom girl and I continued down a path that grew dim. I had passed this park a few times before. it was always filled with health conscious joggers and mothers watching their children enjoy the outdoors.

Allan....

Please....not....now

"Used to come here as a kid. But there's been reports of a lot of gang activity. Drug related stuff." I could tell she was trying her hardest to strike up a friendly conversation and damned if I didn't want to engage in one.

"Really?"

She let off a sort of smile. "Yeah. A guy was mugged a few weeks ago by a large group of teens. It happened again but by a different set of kids. It's got me worried."

> *She wants to take you from me.*
> You're crazy
> *She won't let us be together*
> I'm just walking her home
> *She won't let us be together!*

Carrie's voice was so bitter and it scratched my inner thoughts. I was afraid I was wearing all my nervousness on my face. It was a mask, no, a truth about how my inner mind was a mess. A dream girl, stuck at the bottom of my poisoned well. A clueless woman trying her hardest to show her affection.

It's hanging on the brim of her eyes. Warm, beautiful eyes.

> *She wants you to herself*

I ignore the mind woman. She's only a figment. Carrie the girl I could never obtain.

You...can't leave me...

The angel speaks softly in the moonlight. She tells me of how she walked in on Mr. Strum and Claire, the secretary, doing the horizontal tango.

"I got a raise." she laughs.

I do too. Her color is inviting, pulsating. I'm drawn to her. Away from my thoughts. Loose and untamed. The air picks up and caresses my back. She pulls in closer. There's no resistance.

We slowly approach the exit gates. Bold and haunting the large iron bars call to me. I feel like running. Something deep inside me tells me to. To get out before....

"There's the Lover's Wishing Well." We stop as she points it out.

I look over. My eyes well up with icy tears. Mind all a clutter with the constant dreams, the reality, and my own self doubts.

This woman was giving me her full attention. I loved it. But a furious wave of fear shook me. Maybe she was just looking for sex. Like all the others. Or worse, she just wanted a walk home. Nothing more.

I refused to think this tension be only a walk. The thought sat suspended on my brow.

With her loving hand now on mine, she pulled me toward the stone structure. Moss covered and forgotten it lay off to the side of the exit.

No…please, Allan….
<u>Shut up. This is reality.</u>
NO! She'll just leave you.

She smiles and her eyes catch the moon. My heart skips a beat. Time is but a figment.

"I used to come to this well when I was a kid."

"Me too."

Another smile. "Then you know how it works?"

I don't. I remember as a kid a girl took me here. We played a game and made a wish. No recollection of a story behind it or any reason. Then again as kids, did anything ever matter?

"Refresh my memory."

A warm laugh. "Well this isn't any old well. It's the lover's wishing well. When it was built, the artist carved a heart in every stone. It was a sign of devotion to his wife. That year she was killed by a rare skin disease."

I'm real Allan…I'm real

I quiet her voice as much as possible.

She's a slut….

"What happened to the man?" I ask, only half intrigued. This whole moment felt right. Like time was vibrating softly in the distance.

"Some say he took his life and now rests at the bottom of the well."

I cough. That's a little disturbing to think people gather at a well where someone may be rotting.

Don't let me rot…

"So you can't make wishes?" I say looking into the dark void.

She takes a seat on the ledge. "Only ones of love."

It's a little old fashioned but right now it feels sweet. Her voice speaking of hope and love.

I'm down here Allan….

Her voice now distinct. Almost alive.

Look at me...

Something moves just at the bottom. I shake myself into thinking it's just a reflection. My heart now in rapid beats.

"I made a wish when I was a kid."
I'm back to where I was before. Back to that dark thinking. The dream and the unreachable love. No real emotion. No beating heart to feel with.

Only Carrie.
Allan......
The woman continues her tale of her first kiss.
Allan....

The voice scratching at my mind. A toxin demanding attention. Again I was overwhelmed with thought. Too many directions for me to go. Doubt welling up, dark as the well I'm gazing into for answers.
"Allan?"
Her hand on my back.
Allan!
"Allan..."

Do I succumb to passion? Kiss her like she so easily led me to do? Do I continue in my delusion? Look for Carrie at the bottom of this well? Will I ever be happy? is this only a kiss? Does this mean nothing? Do I mean anything to anyone?
"Allan."
Allan
"Allan?"
Allan!
"Allan...answer me."
Allan!!
"Allan are you alright?"
Allan!
"Allan!"
Fear and tension.
Allan!
Love and loathing.

"Allan! It's not funny!"
Allan!
Fear. Love.
"Allan!"
Anger.
I just need to breath.
Alan look at me!

"God, Damn It!"

My hands around flesh. Tight. Pulling away this monster's breath. No more dreaming, no screams to haunt me. I was ending it. Killing the thought.

Moonlight in her eyes and reality quakes. Carrie was no dream. This was Carrie O'Brian. Her glossed over blues now gazing at me with the same fear I had. The girl of my dreams. As my fingers loosen on her neck, she falls back. Into the shadows Carrie tumbles.

Her name had escaped me all night. No. My fear and doubt kept it from me.

Carrie couldn't be real. Not in my reality. She couldn't have eyes for me. Not in my head. Not with all this doubt.

Hot tears fall. They seem to steam with the Autumn cold.

One last breath.

"Allan…"

It's faint.

But I hear it echo from the darkness below.

My heart full of love. Head full of thought, I take that leap.

-END-

WHEN EVIL LIVED THERE

-1-

Somber dreams and poetic visions cascaded out from her grasp. Sara breathed in deep and took in the reality around her. Her tattered room, full of endless piles of clothes and boxes, disgusted her deep. The stench of alcohol and sex still lingered from the night before. Eyes as jaded as the soul found the source of the odor, a twenty-something drummer whom Sara found interesting after several shots of tequila. Don't mistake the logic girl it'll only kill you faster. Sara's heart raced as she located time and was once again imprisoned by agenda. Shifting from bed to floor she gathered her fallen clothes and went to the kitchen.

Brent moved like a fallen branch, weightless to the morning wind. His eyes had a hollowed glaze from the night of drugs and liquor he had experienced. The film reel was jumping into focus but the memories seemed to be ill-placed. Something felt off as Brent's head throbbed with sunny disposition. He heard the approaching creaks from the wooden floor and fell back into false sleep. Gaining control over his breathing, Brent waited silent for Sara to slip back into bed as to scare her when she did so.

Sara crept in like a broken shadow. Her torso twisted through the garbage and forgotten possessions, moving without bones as Sara chanted an inner montra. The cold touch of the blade in her grasp sent slithering phantoms throughout her body. She was no longer in control, again a victim to her growing dementia. Everything fizzled to a shade of red as Sara approached her sleeping Romeo. His bitter breath reached her nostrils, Sara almost gagging at it's peculiar scent.

Everything was falling out of sense and Sara's mind finally had it's curtain. The sharp iron tore through Brent's paper flesh quickly, slashing and jabbing with a doctor's efficiency. His screams fell quiet to the broken ears of his love. Hollow and vacant the shell of Sara continued it's sadistic mutilation. Chunks of soft peach flesh now stained with human emotion flew with grace through the air. The sun from the window illuminated the scene as finally Brent's marrow was revealed.

His perfectly lined spinal cord was sensual in it's macabre display. Sara pressed her fingers across it, a rush of ecstasy coursing through her. This raw emotion woke Sara's consciousness, bringing with it shock and fear. She dropped from the twitching body of her friend and smacked the unforgiving floor with a loud thud. The knife spiraled away from her grasp and sang with metal tone. What was taking hold of her?

Reality hits you hard, every moment you wake up you need to be ready for death. Sara moved from the floor and peered at the grotesque corpse of her one night stand. His back was completely ripped open and his face was contorted in a terrifying manor of utter pain. Tears dripped from their ducts as Sara stared with confusion at her blood stained hands. Again she had committed murder, this time in her own home.

She fled from the room, her left toe grazing the sharpened blade. The tiny cut went unnoticed as Sara tumbled onto the bathroom floor. Releasing the self-loathing and the terror from her lips, Sara screamed into the deep bowl of the toilet. Her vomit danced around and exploded with every new contribution. Forget what you know about yourself Sara, you're not who you think you are.

The voices in her head were getting louder and Sara couldn't handle it. Moving from the fetal position to a strong stance she opened her medicine cabinet. After the first few pills kissed her, she lost track of numbers and soon the orange bottle sat empty in the sink. The reflection in the mirror was a monster, a ghost to the world. It was a reflection Sara didn't recognize as she had never faced it before.

Her usual victims were usually fat men who had paid her for a good time. Their ill-fated bodies brought to the darkest regions of hooker town and added to the growing pile of dead lovers in a hidden river. Sara, or as her dead friends knew her Lola, never remembered killing these men. Each time she awoke from her bizarre states she was standing over their sinking faces in Paul's Sanctum. This safe haven was where all the town's night women dropped off their bad customers.

Cops never came around and no one ever missed them. They were already dead when they slipped the sinful bills between Sara's legs. With a drug-hazed demeanor Sara crossed the hall and once again entered her room. The date on her day calendar reached out with importance. March 6th 2006. The blood that escaped Brent was now on the move across the floor. It was beautiful in it's own sick sense of art. Sara stumbled onto her vanity. She was loosing herself fast to her second crime today and she needed to make her next move immediately. Turning too fast cause Sara to fall into the pond of crimson.

Her laced bra and panties grew cold with her skin as she tried to gain her feet. The paint drizzled from the ground and slowly bathed poor Sara in a mark of murder. She moved barefoot to her front door. All of her sanity gripped the golden handle of the entrance and demanded not to open it. She could clean this and quickly cover it up. Create the wax to cover yourself in, no one will know the difference. It's not like you're not already used to the idea plastic girl with the tainted dreams.

The feeling of doing what was right approached like a stranger. Sara needed to stop these voices, needed to right her wrong and get out of this house. Powerful images of her father and mother blazed with remorse through Sara's dying mind. Past memories were on repeat, moving through her entire existence in one short breath. Sara's slippery grip on the handle turned and the open air from the outside chilled across her pores.

Stepping onto the first step she saw her neighbor from across the street. Her scared face and loud cry was the only thing Sara could focus on as she slowly stepped down each block of cement. Finally reaching the concrete sidewalk Sara silenced the voices. Their echoing nonsense drifting into nothingness. Her breath was rough and dry, her lips cold with death. As more and more people approached Sara fell into the arms of an on looking man.

Looking deep into his blue eyes Sara felt peace wrap around her. She smiled and told the hero, "I...killed..."

Drowned out by screams and gasps the police sirens went almost unnoticed. As police entered the fabled structure Sara's shell was placed in a dark bag. She left the world not knowing that with her exit she would end a thirty year terror. She left the world not knowing that the price she paid for her home was a price birthed from murder. She left the world not knowing that her act of sinful rage was the twenty-ninth death to occur on these grounds. Sara Briars was a killer, a whore, a lost soul but above all she was a hero.

This final act brought with it justice to those who wished this place to be destroyed. No longer would evil seep from every surface and take hold of the people who tried to carve out an existence there. People are evil, places have no convictions. This twisted sense of thinking brought down Sara Briars and those before her. Every life taken was another story to tell, another moment burned into history. Each year from then on the people would have to remember when evil lived there.

-2-

Well if this isn't what the picture had to offer. I could swear the brick's did not look like they needed this much work. I'm less then thrilled about all this but, if it's what he wants. Look at him. He's beautiful isn't he? Lucas, you truly are a great man and I am so lucky to have you. God, I love that wonderful auburn hair of yours. It's so sexy, I just want to pull it. I love running my fingers through your hair. This is a feeling I can sit with forever. Even standing next to you, one hand caressing your neck, the other gripped with anticipation, this feels right.

My mother was an idiot to think that you weren't capable of becoming someone of worth. Remember when we first met? We were much younger then, seniors in high school. Watching you from the opposite side of the bench, the opposing team, our enemy. It was sort of a sexual fantasy of mine, a vice of sleeping with the bad guy. You were the perfect candidate. Quarterback of the football team, so cliché but I wasn't any cheerleader. Just the girl with the camera lens , my looking glass to hide behind. I was full of enough school spirit and pride though to know I hated your guts. All the more reason for me to pursue you.

I remember walking over, taking pictures of the side lines on your school's side. The visiting section was terrible then. It was so small, the paint chipping from the old metal seating. God, someone should have condemned those bleachers. Garbage was everywhere, I got a lot of shots with empty cups and popcorn bags hidden in there somewhere. For some reason you weren't playing in this particular inning. Your alternate or whatever was in for you, giving him some play time. You know I was never good at football.

I laugh, my soft giggle drawing your eyes to meet with mine. The smooth hue of brown that is painted in your iris pulls me in. I'm sinking deep into the clutch of how tragically beautiful you are. Maybe not tragic. Why did I think tragic? You break our moment, I slip back into my previous thought. I'm taking in the sounds but not exactly processing the noise. It's like the buzzing fuzz on a TV set left on in the hollows of my mind. The box just sitting there, haunting almost.

My bright flash shot out, it's flickering call making you my center of attention. Your eyes had the same hypnotic arousal about them that you still trick me with now. We talked, the conversation meaning nothing but strung together words wrapping around you and hopefully leading you to where I wanted you to go. I remember it was a little cold out and you wrapped your arms around me and then quickly moved them when your coach yelled at you.

Your head was suppose to be on the game but I knew that it was lost, void of anything but that brief moment. I waited, resting against the wall facing your team's lockers. My girl friend insisted on waiting, and we both felt the dozens of stares that were locked on us. Tiny of prickling tensions that hurt like quiet gun fire. It was worth every minute, and that was held true the moment you saw me in the small crowd. Where the hell were your parents kid?

I look and realize we're in the kitchen. Not so bad. It's cold, a terrible chill that seems perfectly placed. Almost like a mood setter. Steel. That was the apparent theme that this previous house owner had puked everywhere. So unforgiving, it's mirror surfaces are so persistent. Those reflections lie to me.

"Kitchen's great. I still want to see that bedroom.", Lucas says to the blond relater.

She smiles her cheap smile at you and sells, "Right up these stairs. The second bathroom, full bath, is across the hall."

The clicking of her heels grinds across my brain as she leads us through the house. As her over the top character and plastic shell gets half way up the beautiful staircase, she stumbles. My husband; you go to grab her but you slip too. They cleaned the wooden things much too recently and our shoes are completely weak to it's smooth surface.

Unforgiving, reflecting the terror our relater's fate. Her heels, those foul things that cause pain in the payment for a little height, worked against her and she tumbled over the banister. Every inch of her blond skull shattered against the tile flooring below. It sketched out a horrific image of gruesome accident. I gripped the cold banister as the picture burned out. You turned at my sudden movement and gave me a queer gaze.

Susan, as I believe the lucky bitch was, seemed ignorant to the whole thing. It never happened. I...I imagined it. I just thought I saw. What the fuck is wrong with me? You completely dismissed my tremor but I can't blame you. All you saw was my body tense up. But I felt it.

I could have sworn.

Nothing.

We talked and I lead you.

I remember I had lead you to the bleachers again.

The visitor side was on the far end of the campus, it's back against the first row of neighboring houses. There wasn't much talking when we reached the dark alcove of steel pipes. I was afraid of being cut by rusted tumors or scars that grazed everywhere underneath. You had every inch of me at your whim. I was yours, and my lustful thirst become quenched in an animalistic rush of passion. Cold wind kissed the bare skin on our backs as they appeared in the shallow moonlight. I knew the second your eyes met mine we would end up here. My camera's focus catching that thirst in your eyes too.

You appear at the end of the small hall. I can see that perfect grin that you have painted on your chin. The sales woman knows she has you and being our first home feels wonderful. I have no objections. To long have we had to feel comfort in a shit apartment we paid too much for. A promotion? And you're headlining your first build. I have never been more proud of you. My lips grow course as the thirst begins to well inside me. The parasite of sexual tension winds tighter in the pit of my stomach.

I can hear the two of you discussing payments or closing, signing the papers. Whatever it is you do to get this place. This is our home now and it's perfect. There is a looming omnipresent feeling that keeps this hall slightly unsettled. As you approach I catch the end of your conversation.

"We hope to complete our main frame work by the end of 2000. It's very exciting."

Susan smiles and hands over paper to Lucas. "Well I would say so. This home is a steal and I'm glad the two of you are interested. This place could use a young couple or two."

I approach and clutch your arm. As I stand and stare at this woman's face I remember a newspaper article I had found online. This address brought up some bizarre sites on the vast web. One seemed to be important. The clipping had a man, his old face center in a dark window. He was glossed and vacant. My mind pulls for the title but the woman's chatter makes it hard.

You're trying to close the deal but I still say I remember this article. The title. What the fuck was the title?

I suddenly blurt out, a phantom whisper, "When evil lived there."

The words felt so cold as they slipped past my lips. Their dead corpses waiting restlessly in the air. Lucas, you step closer to me, your breath sweet against my neck. I felt so unsure about this house that I looked it up. I was obsessed. Afraid almost. The hidden tremble my body was suspended in was getting worse as the silence of the hall way lingered on. The relater looked at us and smiled politely. How fake your smile is you bitch. I want to rip out your jaws and stomp against it's bleeding marrow again and again.

My shakes gain their breaking point and I do a small stumble. Weak like paper my legs give out and I rest in Lucas's arms. "Sorry." I manage to say.

"Don't worry about it. But, what did you say before?" You say as you help me to my feet.

"There was a newspaper article. The title read..."

Susan cuts in," 'When Evil Lived There' "

I feel the warmth of your body move away from me. You cross before me and move in to question Susan. The grey of your shirt looks brilliant in the high lights on the hall. With my palm I trace your spine, feeling the smooth ridges as it trails down your back. Suddenly I feel warm liquid. It's rich thickness calling attention to it's soft crimson color. How beautiful your torso looks with the elegant cuts that blaze across it's surface. The blood trickles over my fingers and I feel a warmth grow inside me.

Your voice pulls me away from the feeling. The visions scatter out, their tiny apparitions dancing into nothing. I look up and catch your eyes and smile. There is a quiet hum that floats through my ear drums. What the fuck was I thinking? I choose to ignore the visions and move next to you. Susan looks bothered and concerned with our questions. It's written in black ink across her worn skin. Her smile an added touch to the already crumbling mess of having to confront something that may be hard to speak of.

"What do you mean something happened here?"

She crosses her hands and replies, "It pains me to tell you but people were murdered in this house. Now the interior design and lay out has been heavily remodeled since then. Besides the stone walls around us and the dirt below our feet, nothing of those terrible crimes remain here."

"Cut the shit and tell us what happened", I force out.

You look at me and I can tell your glare carries heavy weight. The writing on Susan's face twists into a darker markings of despair. I can't believe I blurted that out. This awkward preposition reminds me of when I was younger. My parents were always throwing around curse words and ignoring any sense of morality. I picked up the habit and realized how terrible it was only when I started dating you. It was like I got a sort of rush from using offensive language.

I hear the rustling of Susan's suit coat and look in her direction.

"A few years back, when this place went up for a sale a man from Texas came up and bought it on the spot. The man was so enthusiastic about the move he seemed to be over powered with joy. That's why it was all the move shocking when they made the discovery of the first body."

Her words become hazy as I stand and try to listen. The first body? History is what separates reality from fantasy. A place having history, horrific or not, breathes life into it. Reality is placed within time, time turning into history. Always being history while fantasy exists in parallel times and places. Time has no hold over them as they do over us. The tales are figments, strung together moments void of true life.

My head feels heavy with dread and carrying on with the conversation. This place has me, holds me, making me feel at home. Lucas, you may have been the only person in our duo to want the place but now that I stand on it's oak floors I just feel right. The looming phantom of something dark arouses my senses. It pulls at the tiny specks of my flesh, it haunts my mind, a winding destruction I sense I'm lusting for.

Susan's words break my thought. She says, "During a neighborly visit, the woman who lived across from him saw blood on a few of the door handles and on the railings of the staircase. When the cops came to look into the older woman's assumptions they found the body of the Texas man's daughter in the closet. After a few months of digging around they found the body of the wife in the attic space."

"Body parts." Again I shake as the words tumble out.

You shoot your glare towards me and then back at Susan. I can see you're confused on whether to ignore my outburst again or to address it. I don't believe I used enough breath to make it audible to anyone around me. It was just so sudden and unexpected. The phantom drifted closer and I cold feel the sweet breath of his against my neck.

"Yes. Once Mr. Larson's journals were read deeper they found confessions of hiding the body parts of other victims in the furniture of the house. In all 5 people died at the hands of this man. But again, this was twenty or so years ago and the house has drastically changed." The false tone of her voice cracked as it sounded out. How plastic and useless the last statement now seemed.

Your voices go silent as time wears on. The very moment she stopped speaking it was as if someone had hit me in the back of my skull. The hum in my ears turned into a distant buzz that stung like acid. Papers flew and things were signed and I coast through movements of thanking dear Susan for the tour. The rush of the wind against my face brings the buzzing to a peaceful low.

I feel the tender grip of your hands as they meet with my shoulders.

"I think I'm going to like it here."

Turning to face you I say, "Terrible thing that happened."

"Doesn't matter. I'm not too worried about it. Are you?"

As the wind presses with more force I swear it's hollowed breath speaks. It whispers with distant words that gathers within it's grasp. And as the words gain their weight and their truths made clear I swear I hear a voice quietly speaking to the dirt, *When evil lived there.*

I stood there, looking out the window, leg rested on that maroon and dirt soaked futon. This place is so full of life. The street alive with neighbors walking dogs, talking with one another as they drink cups of coffee. I like it here. But I don't like this house. As I'm standing here, looking out the window, I feel a chill. It grows from the bottom of my back, slowly soothing over my shoulders. I feel it's cold grip wrap around my neck. It slowly caresses my flesh, I'm a victim to it's touch. I shake myself. Lucas? When are you coming home?

I return to the kitchen to finish carving the meat. Couldn't tell you what I was making if you asked. Halfway past my madness I forgot the recipe, not that it mattered. The quiet crackle of the boiling water reminded me about the finished noodles. I'll serve it up with the cooked meat, some sauce I bought before and hand it to you. Hope you like it. I never was a good cook was I?

I leave the carving board and enter the dinning room. I try to admire the photos you hung on the walls. My photos, so thoughtful. Fucking bastard. You chose the worst ones, the ones I hate. I tell you again and again that these are my worst photos. Somehow you find ways of shoving them down my throat. Giving them as gifts or even, hanging them on the walls of my own god damn house!

The scenes of tonight's dinner play out in my head. You sit across from me, the anecdote about your work slipping past your lips. I smile and look down at the tainted plate before me. The noodles release somber phantoms of steam. I raise my glass of wine and swallow hard. It's bitter taste blazes across my taste buds. My hand grips the cold utensil left forgotten. I stand up, fork in hand, walk over to you. I look into your eyes lovingly as I caress the back of your neck. Then I feel the sudden gale from the silver flying through the wind.

It's sharp prongs meeting with the flesh of your throat, a sea of crimson dancing onto the poorly made poison. I rip the weapon from your voice and drive it one more time into your eye. A thick ooze seeps out with the blood, my hands painted with it's sin. You scream out in pain but it's only failed grasps. It sounds like the dying wind of a great tornado. The echo of your breath fading away with the scene.

I leave the dining room and return to the kitchen. My eyes only linger on our dinner for a moment. Why am I thinking like this? These wicked images that pulse throughout my reality course through me. Each moment another wave of sudden and dark excitement. I stumble to the fridge and retrieve a can of soda. I feel the acidic fuzz foam across my tongue and throat. What is wrong with me.

The doorbell rings. I ignore it. There's a knock and I ignore it. Who the fuck would be coming over at this time?

I look across to the dining room and I see him.

I see you. Who are you and why do sit at the table? Are you hungry? You turn and look at me, your dead eyes burning. I feel their empty blackness rip into my soul, my feet melting into the floor. Your jaw. Where is your jaw? The blood dripping over the wood panels beneath your feet. Go away!

There's a knock at the door. I ignore it but I slip near the window to see who is trying to reach me. Susan. What could she want? We bought the house a little over two months ago. The hell do you want? I leave for the kitchen and turn off the noodles and the sizzling meat. My hands shake as they rest on the smooth counter tops.

My ears sit in silence as I wait for the sound of your keys sliding into the locks. I need to get my mind off of these evil thoughts. The darkness of my deeds pull close to my body. I can feel your macabre touch soothe over my back and my legs. I move my trembling hand and slip it into my skirt. My wicked fingers find the entrance of my womanhood, the haunting breath of shadowed thoughts taking hold.

Before I know it I hear your keys enter the door handle. The echo of my heated orgasm tumbles out into the empty kitchen. I adjust myself and realize I need to heat the tomato sauce. The rosy substance falls into a white container. I hear you talk but I don't understand what you're saying. You enter the kitchen with your perfect smile on display. I kiss you, your lips taste so stale. An omnipresent after taste of mud.

"Dinner isn't ready yet."

You laugh, 'That's ok. I can wait."

The deep foots steps lead you to the living room where you sit before the TV and watch your final program. I continue to stand before the apathetic meal I'm barely keeping an eye on. My hands rub the edge of the counters and lead my to the sink. One hand slips under to the cabinet and retrieve the container of blue ingredient. It floods out, leaping out over the cold sauce and the hard noodles. I quickly pull together two plates and two glasses of your favorite wine.

I take it over, all of the tainted perfection and place it elegantly at the empty table. As I finish placing my seat you step in and sit down. Your smile warms my anger and pulls at my sorrow. I take the single chair and grab the metal fork in my hand. I laugh as I stare at the lie, toying with it as if it were you flesh. My sharp prongs stabbing at it.

I hear the serenade of the phantoms sing out. This house is alive with death. And I feel it's dark harshness dance across my body. It grips me so. I've gone truly mad. I feel the serenade sing out again and again. Me and you toast as I play with the noodles. You take that first bite.

I watch as again and again you shovel my waxy death down your throat. You barely taste it's poison. I raise my glass of wine and that's when everything gets hazy.

From your dying coughs to the police sirens echoing out, it blurs with time. I called them. But did I want to be caught? I dance with the thought as they put me in handcuffs. I feel their cold steel twist around my wrists, I cry as I'm placed in the back of the swat car. I'm free. I don't feel your presence within me. You no longer have hold over me. As I'm now a block away I see you. I see you glaring out. The windows your eyes, the door your smile. I'm free. The unforgiving faceless structure you manifest in grows small. As I sit I recall the first thing I heard in the broken wind.

It's phantom voice fading as the distance between us sinks in. I hear it, as it cries out, "When evil lived there."

-3-

wake up and feel him standing there.
above me.
staring down at me.
eyes on me.
when no one else is there.
he stands above me.
my mother sees him not.
my dad says he's not real.
but it's his eyes I feel.
piercing into me
in my dreams.
in my wake.
no peace. no break.
in the corner watching.
in the corner crying.
in the dark. all alone.
no one to turn to.
no one to ask for help.

do you believe me?
do you feel his breath as I do?
he's standing now.
he's here now.
my parents, no.
they're quieted now.
silenced. just me.
and him.

he's here with me.
his eyes against my back.
in my soul.
he believe me.

he knew he was there.
he was always there.
when no one else was.

when evil lived here...

-suicide note; Elizabeth Summers.
found next to her body, written in the blood of her mutilated
parents.

thank you for reading this collection of short horror fictions.

in purchasing this book you are giving life to a penniless writer's

dream, and I cannot thank you enough.

look for more short story collections and books coming soon.

not always to invoke the emotion of fear.
soon there will be love.
and sorrow.
and joy.

but there will always be passion.
for at it's strongest, all emotion becomes passion.

www.ingramcontent.com/pod-product-compliance
Lightning Source LLC
Chambersburg PA
CBHW060127260626
47160CB00005B/2038